CAUSED BY DRAY

BILLIONAIRE DRAY ROYCE SERIES #9

SHEILA MURDOCK

ALSO AVAILABLE IN PAPERBACK

ALSO BY SHEILA MURDOCK

DIVESTED
Crystal
THE DIVESTED BWWM SERIES
SHEILA MURDOCK
The Vain Society
SHEILA MURDOCK
Entitled Woman
SHEILA MURDOCK
LAVONNE ON THE JOB
The Hair Salon
SHEILA MURDOCK
HIS Mess HIS Stress
A NOVEL
SHEILA MURDOCK
LESSONS Lisa
SHEILA MURDOCK
Billionaire Bliss
SHEILA MURDOCK
THE Club
A NOVEL
SHEILA MURDOCK
STANDALONES and STANDALONE SERIES
MORE to COME!

NIGHT SKY AFFAIR: TABITHA IS COMING SOON IN 2024

I'm
Sleeping
With Your
Husband
A NOVEL
WHEN THE UNEXPECTED
BECOMES
EVEN MORE UNEXPECTED
SHEILA
MURDOCK
STANDALONES
MORE to COME!

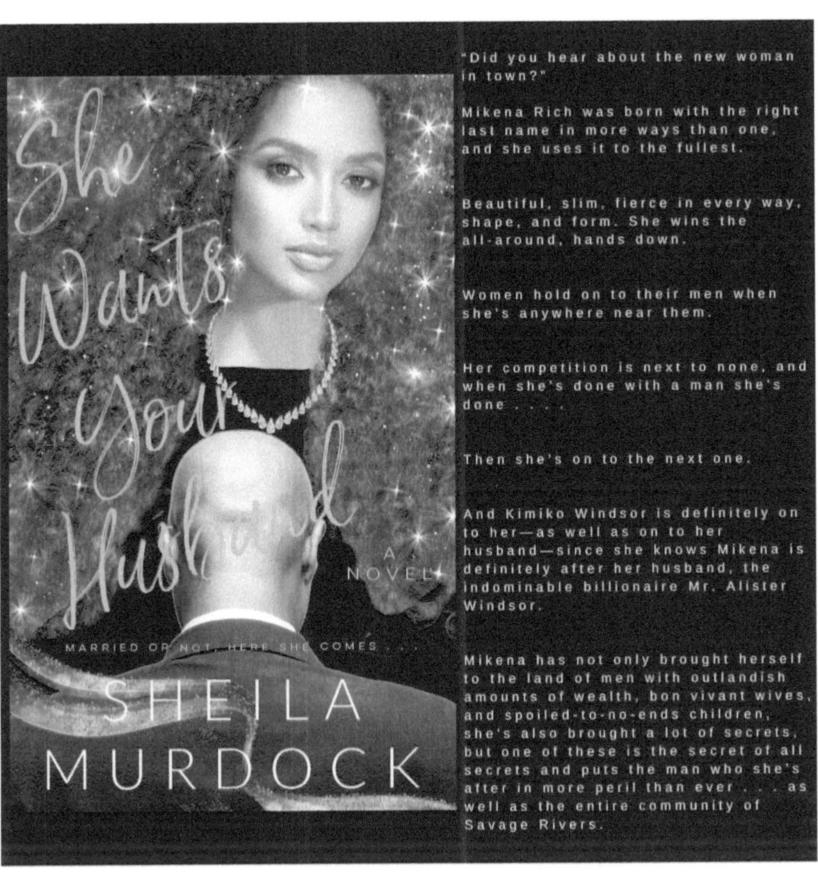

SHE WANTS YOUR HUSBAND - COMING SOON

"You have everything, man! *Everything!* You have all the money, a beautiful wife and kids, looks, status, and power that you want! Why are you always causing bad shit to happen? *Why?*"

— CHIEF SMITH

CONTENTS

CHAPTER 1

THE PATRIARCH

THE WROUGHT IRON GATES SLOWLY OPENED TO THE FRONT entrance of Dray's and my house as the media was blocked by a wall of cops and our personal security as they already shouted questions at us and fought with each other while trying to get the best spots available before we even got a chance to speak about this latest incident this morning. But this was one we all never saw coming, but as usual there was a strong connection to us because of it which was why we needed to speak on it.

"Are you all ready?" Todd asked us.

"Yes," we all replied.

I held Layton as I shook my head while still wearing my outfit from Lulu's garden party. Lulu and Miriam hadn't changed either and we weren't even thinking about it. I felt like it'd been hours since we'd been there and I could see the mental anguish all over Lulu's face about what was going on, but the last thing she was thinking about was the fact that her party had been interrupted because there was something much more important than that which we were all very much concerned with and rightfully so, because no one ever had to face this in Royce family history . . . twice.

Todd walked up to the microphones as Clayton stood behind him with Lulu on his right side and Dray on his left side. Miriam stood back next to me as Carmella stood right next to her as she held Stormy. Our bodyguards stood all around us.

"Thank you all for being here this morning. As you all know, there are three women who escaped from jail this morning and two of them have a connection to the Royce family. But what we're concerned with is that the Royce family patriarch, Mayson Royce, is missing and has not been heard from since early this morning. All attempts to contact him from his family right here to friends and former colleagues have been unsuccessful. We have no idea of his whereabouts at this moment. I'm going to turn it over to Clayton Royce, Mayson's son," Todd said, and stepped out of the way.

Clayton cleared his throat as he stood with his arm around his mother while Dray still stood by his side. "Like Mr. Johnson just informed you all, my dad is missing. Never has this ever happened before to him and there are no words to describe how I'm feeling and how we're all feeling right now. We just want him back here with us. There are just too many ways to contact people now and too much people can find out, and we haven't found out a damn thing as to where my dad is at this moment. You all know who he is and what he looks like and we want him back with us. I will not disclose any information about any reward money at this time. My mom wants to say something."

Lulu stood in front of the microphones as the flashes from the cameras were almost blinding. "I'm Lulu Royce. The matriarch of the Royce family. My husband is Mayson Royce, the patriarch. We have been married for well over 70 years now, and ever since I've known him, this has never happened before. He will be 95 years old this year. He did not just wander off because he is in his right state of mind. He knew about my party and he usually goes to Grayson's with his friends while my party is going on. He was not there so I don't know where he is. I have not seen or heard from him since this morning before my party started. Please help us find him."

Clayton comforted her as they stood back to let Dray speak next.

Dray sighed as he shook his head. I knew this was very difficult for him. "I'm Dray Royce. My gramps means everything to me just like the rest of my family. As you all know, we have never been put in this situation before when it comes to him. He's always been responsible and always aware. We just don't know where he is right now. I feel like it was just yesterday that my beautiful wife Eve and my kids were missing, and now it's my gramps. We need everyone on this to help us find him. Like my dad said, no information about reward money will be disclosed at this time because we don't want any false leads. Thank you."

Todd walked back up to the podium. "As you all see on your phones and other devices, the contact information is all on there as well as his picture if any of you out there have any information about the whereabouts of Mayson Royce, the Royce family patriarch. We won't be answering any questions. Thank you."

But in classic media fashion, Todd stating that we weren't answering any questions went through one ear and out the other as they shouted questions anyway as the wrought iron gates closed in front of them and we all walked back up to the house as I could feel my dress fading from all of the lights of the flashes from cameras on my back as Dray had his arm around me. I looked up at him as he stared straight ahead, and never had I ever seen him look so sad and worried before, and I knew he'd looked like this when Layton and I were missing, as well as Stormy.

We all settled into the family room as the TV showed live news coverage of the escaped inmates as well as now Mayson being missing as Breaking News.

"He has a phone. I just wish he would call us," Lulu said as tears streamed from her eyes as Miriam was now comforting her as they sat on one of the sofas.

"And that's why I'm worried because he does have a phone and he hasn't called us," Clayton said in a cracked voice, and I'd never seen him looked so worried before as him and Dray stood over the couch.

I sat in a separate chair as I still held Layton as he slept soundly in my arms as Carmella still held Stormy as she sat on another sofa. I just didn't know what to say or what to think. I didn't expect any of this, but it was clear that wherever Mayson was, someone didn't want us to know that he was with them until they probably got the oldest thing in the book . . . Money.

"Dray," Auer said.

"What, man?" Dray replied in a defensive tone.

"Brock and Jose are here," Auer informed him.

We all looked at each other since they'd told Dray they were on vacation, but they obviously were still in the area since they were able to get back here so fast.

Brock and Jose walked into the family room to Dray giving them his patented daunting stare.

"Hey," Brock managed to squeak out.

"Hey, nothing!" Dray said.

"Dray," I said in calm voice. "Please stay calm."

Dray stared the two of them down. "What's going on? Y'all know where my gramps is? Because we haven't been able to find him for well over two hours now and no one has seen or heard from him since he left my grandmother this morning."

"No, man, we don't know," Jose informed him.

"We really don't, man," Brock said.

We all stared at Dray to see what else he was going to say because I could tell by their responses that they were telling the truth.

Jose sighed. "I don't know if this is gonna help or not."

Everyone gasped!

"What? What is gonna help or not?!" Dray asked him as he got all up in his face. Auer and Leon slightly pushed him back from him.

Jose sighed once again. "You called me, man, about Ellesse? Remember?"

We all gasped once again!

"YES! Of course I remember! You know where she is? Does it have something to do with my gramps?"

Brock and Jose looked at each other.

Jose sighed for like the hundredth time as his head hung low. "I don't know about your gramps, man, but we put Ellesse in your gramps's yacht."

"WHAT?!" Dray yelled as we all gasped in shock! "WHAT?!"

"He's telling the truth, Dray, we did," Brock confirmed. "We didn't want her getting away and telling on you about whatever your involvement is with her."

"I have no fuckin' involvement with her!"

"Drayton!" Miriam said.

I sighed as I shook my head. I looked up to find Leon staring right at me.

Clayton got on his phone. "I'm calling Vernon Baucus to have my dad's yacht checked out. Chances are she's probably still there."

"She should be. We locked her in there where she couldn't get out," Brock said.

"Get the fuck out of here, you two. I don't know what the hell I wanna do with the both of you right now," Dray said.

Brock and Jose looked at each other.

"GO!" Dray barked as he pointed in the direction of the front door.

Layton and Stormy screamed in tears.

"Auer, Leon, make sure they leave," Dray said, and then sat down on the couch next to me and cupped his hands as he buried his face in them.

I looked at him as I could tell he was trying very hard not to lose it about all of this, and we didn't even know if Ellesse really was where Jose and Brock claimed that she was. "Dray. I don't think they're lying to you. If they say she's there then chances are she's still there." I got up and sat on the sofa with him. I handed Layton to him. Carmella got up off the other sofa and handed Stormy to him.

Tears streamed down his face as he held his children as he looked at the TV which showed pictures and videos of Mayson since we'd confirmed that he was missing. "This is not how I want my kids to remember their great-grandfather. This is not his legacy."

"And they won't remember his legacy as being a missing man, Dray, because we will find him," I assured him, even though there was no way I could be a hundred percent about it.

Clayton hung up with Vernon as he came back into the room. "The cops are on their way to his yacht. He told us all to stay here. He's gonna have someone with him livestreaming everything so we can see what's going on."

"What about my husband? Your father?" Lulu asked as Miriam still tried to comfort her.

Clayton lowered his head. "I don't know, Mom. You know we got all the cops who are available in the area looking for him." He looked at Dray. "Dray, come here for a second."

Dray handed his kids back to me and Carmella, and went off with his dad. Minutes later, they came back in the room.

I looked at him as he sat back down next to me. "What did the two of you talk about?"

Dray sighed. "I'll tell you if it's true."

CHAPTER 2
THE ESCAPEES

"Okay, Rebecca, we're not fucking around with you. You need to tell us if anyone else is on this yacht because this motherfucker is way too big for there not to be anyone else on it. We all know you're that old, raggedy man's mistress, but there's no way you're on here by yourself. You got your young lover on here, don't you?" Joanna Woodburn said, as she held a gun at Rebecca as her and Ellesse sat on a couch next to each other.

"No, I don't have a young lover," Rebecca said as tears streamed down her eyes.

"So, you're actually the mistress of that old man?" Brittney Hart asked with a huge grin.

"Yes I am. Everyone knows it; it's no secret," Rebecca said. "Could y'all please just let us go? I know Ellesse told you all she's pregnant."

"And?" Brittney said with a grin.

"Yeah, really!" Joanna said as she still pointed the gun at them.

"Who are you pregnant by?" Gina asked.

Everyone looked at Ellesse, including Rebecca.

"Dray," Ellesse informed them.

They all shrieked as they laughed as Rebecca tried not to look surprised.

"You know you're gonna get your motherfuckin' ass kicked by Eve, right?" Gina said, as she sat in a chair facing Ellesse and Rebecca.

"She knows I'm pregnant by him," Ellesse told her.

"And that's probably why you ended up down in here, huh?" Gina said.

Rebecca looked at Ellesse.

"I don't know why I was put in here, okay? Could you all just please let us go? I've been down in here long enough," Ellesse pleaded.

"Nah, we can't let you go—or you either, Rebecca—just yet. We need to do some negotiations with the Royces since we're on one of their yachts," Joanna said.

"What do you want from them? What did they do to you?" Rebecca asked.

"You mean that raggedy-ass, limp-dick bastard you're fucking didn't tell you?" Joanna asked.

Brittney laughed while Gina grinned.

"Please don't disrespect him like that," Rebecca said.

"Girl, you don't even want me to get into how disrespectful your piece-of-shit, wrinkled-old, deflated-balls lover is," Joanna said. "It's clear you haven't heard."

"Haven't heard what?" Rebecca asked.

Everyone looked at Joanna.

"Your billionaire bastard old-as-fuck lover is a murderer," Joanna informed her.

"What?!" Rebecca replied in genuine shock. "You're lying!"

Joanna raised the gun back up at her as she got up and pointed it right to her head!

Ellesse shrieked in panic!

"Don't you *ever* call me a motherfuckin' liar again, you fuckin' whore! Of course you don't give a shit about who you're fucking and sucking in secret because he's keeping you in a lifestyle you would never have otherwise. Mayson Royce is a fuckin' murderer. He had my sister murdered 40 years ago because his bastard married son Clayton got her pregnant. That baby was Clayton's, and they both knew it, so they had her murdered!" Joanna said. She looked at Ellesse. "And if you're really pregnant by Dray then you better be damn lucky you were put in here instead of out there in that water weighed down with weights."

"I'm sorry about your sister, Joanna, but it has nothing to do with Dray," Ellesse said.

"Bullshit. That motherfucker got all of his ways from his dad and granddad, and bitches like you are too stupid to realize it. He ain't ever gonna leave that Eve chick for you or for anyone, just like how his dad never left that Miriam bitch for my sister. You're fighting a losing battle and like I said, you're way too stupid to realize it." She sat back down next to Gina while still holding the gun.

"Is there anyone else on this yacht?" Gina asked, clearly trying to change the subject.

Rebecca sighed as she stared down at her lap.

"Rebecca, you only have one last chance to tell me or I'm sending the two of them to check this place out. So if you're lying to me about no one being on here and we find someone or some people, then you, her, and them are all being weighted down and going overboard," Gina threatened.

Ellesse looked at Rebecca as tears welled up in her eyes.

Gina grabbed the gun from Joanna and pointed it at Rebecca! "Last chance to tell me."

Rebecca raised her hands in the air as Ellesse's eyes told her just how scared she was as tears flowed down hard from them. She knew her life—as well as Ellesse's—depended on how she answered her.

"Brittney, Joanna, go have a look around. This is a big-ass yacht so it may take you a while to check this whole place out. And whoever you find, bring them down here," Gina said as she still glared at Rebecca.

"Please," Rebecca pleaded.

"Please, what?" Gina asked. She shook her head. "Go on, you two. You got the other gun, Brittney, right?"

Brittney pulled out another gun! "Got it."

"Maybe we should stay together since I don't know my way around here since we only have one gun between us," Joanna suggested.

"Good idea," Gina said. "Start at the top out on that deck then just work y'alls way back down here."

"You got it," Brittney said, and her and Joanna left on their search for anyone else who could've been on this yacht.

They stopped by a room that had a sign on the outside: EMPLOYEES LOUNGE.

"*Another* employees lounge?" Brittney asked.

"That's what it says," Joanna said, and twisted the doorknob as Brittney held the gun towards the door . . . .

It opened!

"Shhh!" Joanna said, as she looked side-to-side and then entered the room with Brittney right by her side. "Looks like there's no one here, but let's make sure."

They crept quietly around the room looking for anyone who could've been in here. There was no one in sight.

"Joanna! Look!" Brittney said, and pointed to another room inside of this room that had a closet full of employee uniforms.

"Wow," Joanna said with a huge grin. "Find your size, girl!"

They laughed as they rummaged through the uniforms in search for their size.

Minutes later, they were dressed as Mayson Royce's yacht employees, wearing light blue short-sleeved polo shirts embroidered with *Royce II* in gold on the upper left side along with tan knee-length shorts, and went back on their search to find any employees or anyone else wandering around this yacht.

"Damn this boat is fuckin' huge!" Joanna said as they made their way towards the stairs after having trouble finding them at first, and along the way, they never ran into anyone.

"Yeah, this is the damn life. It's amazing that my so-called mom could've easily had one of these all for having my younger sister by Dray."

Joanna looked at her as they walked up the stairs. "I'm surprised you're calling her your little sister."

"Well, I'm glad that she's alive and I hope that Dray does let me meet her someday because it's not her fault what my triflin'-ass, so-called mom did. You know I don't even call her my mom because I never considered her it because of what she did and it's her fault she's dead. She made me do it."

"I understand, and it's Mayson's and Clayton's fault as to why my older sister is dead. I never really got to know her. I was only 10 years old when it happened. Now I'm 50 years old and a jail escapee. My life just got so fucked up after what'd happened to Jolene, and I vowed to get revenge on the Royce men because of it. It's amazing how connected we could be and it's all because of the Royce men, and none of us will ever live this good."

"Well, Angela came close because she had a baby by Dray and acted as if she wasn't my mom and didn't wanna share her wealth with me that she was supposed to get from him. Had she even shared one percent of it with me, I knew she would've felt some kind of guilt and shame for what she did to me—but she didn't. Damn, what a fuckin' selfish-ass bitch. She really didn't give a shit about me, only about Stormy and what she was able to almost get from Dray for having her. I say *almost* because the mean, wicked-old nasty-ass bitch is dead, and all by my hands."

"I'm so sorry, Brittney. That is fucked up. No one should've gone through the shit you went through. You're only in your early 20s; I have three kids in their 20s and all of them have kids. I have two in their 30s and they have kids as well. Your life should just be beginning and now you're standing next to me, a 50-year-old grandmother being a jail escapee and standing on the yacht of one of the old fuckin' farts who had my older sister killed. You can't make this shit up."

Brittney smiled. "You can't."

"And like what you said about Angela, I try to imagine how Jolene's life would've been had the Royce men let her live. I know they had her killed, Brittney, I know it."

"I believe you."

"They had enough money to pay her off back then, and they have especially enough money to still keep paying her off now. My niece or nephew could and should be 40 years old with his or her own family and we could all be living like this—but not as rich as the Royces, of course—all because of my sister, but they chose to have her and unborn child killed instead. They've done so much evil shit to people, Brittney. We don't even know the half of it."

"Yeah, I believe that. But I took care of Angela for them."

Joanna stopped at the top of the steps. She looked at her "You *what?*"

"I said what I said," she said with a wicked grin. "Dray knows damn well he didn't wanna pay Angela $850 million dollars over the next 18 years with that being $47 million dollars a year. Who the fuck would? He knows what he wanted done with Angela, so I did it."

Joanna kept looking at her as they continued to walk around the top deck.

"Wow! What a top deck! It looks like a cruise ship up here!" Brittney said with true amazement. "Check out the size of that pool!"

"Yeah, this is pretty dope. And what the fuck can a 90-something-year-old man do with all of this? *You know* he's got more than one Rebecca running around here."

"And if we find her—*BANG!*" Brittney said, and held the gun up in the air as if she was gonna fire a shot.

"Don't shoot!" Joanna said as she laughed. "We can't have anything attracting anyone here since no one knows we're here. Let's have a look around."

They walked around checking out this top deck which had all of the luxury amenities one could ever want and dream of.

"Wait!" Joanna said, as they turned a corner to a lounge area.

"What?" Brittney asked as she stood behind her.

"Oh, shit!" Joanna said with complete disbelief. "I see someone!"

"What?!" Brittney said again with her eyes big.

"Someone is sitting on that couch in front of that theater-sized TV! Oh my god! *I knew* someone else was on here, but I can't see them from the front. Stay behind me and put your gun where they can't see it," she whispered.

"Got it," Brittney replied, and put the gun in the pocket of the shorts she was wearing.

They quietly approach the person sitting on the couch. Joanna motioned for Brittney to stay quiet. They noticed that the person was really into watching what was on TV. They looked at each other, and then slowly came around to the front of the couch . . . .

To Mayson being sound asleep!

They looked at each other once again as they held mischievous grins.

"Mr. Royce?" Joanna said.

No answer.

"Mr. Royce?" Brittney said.

No answer.

They looked at each other.

"Oh, no!" Brittney said.

Joanna let out a deep sigh. "Mr. Royce?" she said louder, and then shook him.

Mayson jumped in his seat and took a hard, right arm swing at her!

They shrieked as they jumped back!

"Rebecca?" he asked with his eyes halfway opened.

Joanna and Brittney looked at each other.

"No, Mr. Royce. We're not Rebecca. We work here, see," Joanna said, and pulled on the left side of her top to show the *Royce II* logo.

"Oh. Okay," Mayson said, and closed his eyes again.

They gave each other a confused look.

"Mr. Royce, we were told we have to take you downstairs to Rebecca," Brittney said.

Mayson started snoring again.

"Come on, get up," Joanna said, and forced him on his feet as Brittney helped her with him. "Check his pockets, Brittney."

Brittney searched his pockets and found his phone. "Here's his phone, but he doesn't have it turned on."

"Okay, let's go," Joanna said, as they slowly walked towards the stairs.

Minutes later, they came back into the room with Mayson in tow.

"Look who we found? The Royce patriarch, Mayson Royce!" Joanna announced as she walked Mayson over to sit next to Rebecca.

Gina looked at Rebecca. "How come you didn't tell me he was on here?"

Ellesse looked at Rebecca.

"Because I didn't want you to hurt him," Rebecca honestly replied.

"Who said anything about hurting him?" Gina said.

"Well, you said if they found anyone that we were all gonna be weighted down and thrown overboard," Rebecca reminded her.

Everyone looked at Gina as Mayson smiled with his eyes closed.

"Oh, yeah, I did say that. I forgot just that fast that I did," Gina said. "And what the fuck is he smiling at?"

"He thinks you're attractive," Rebecca said.

"Sugar," Mayson said with his eyes halfway opened.

"Who is he calling sugar?" Gina asked.

"You, Gina. All of you; all of us. Take it as a compliment because he always calls me sugar," Rebecca said.

"Yeah, that's what Clayton told me. Hey, Big May. I fucked your son just like you're fucking Rebecca!" Gina said with a laugh.

Brittney and Joanna laughed hard while Ellesse sat in shock.

"That's not funny, Gina!" Rebecca said.

"Lulu?" Mayson said as he stared at Joanna.

"Lulu?!" Joanna said with disgust. She got up in Mayson's face as she pointed her gun at him.

Rebecca and Ellesse shrieked.

"Do I look like that raggedy-old bitch of yours?! DO I?!" Joanna said.

Gina shook her head with a grin as Brittney laughed.

"Lulu?" Mayson said again.

"Why the fuck does he keep saying that shit?!" Joanna asked Rebecca.

"He's senile!" Rebecca pleaded as tears welled up in her eyes. "Please let us go!"

"No, can't do that just yet," Joanna informed her, and then turned her attention to Mayson. "Why the fuck did you and your son have my sister killed, huh? Didn't want her to live like this from the money your son would've had to pay her off with for keeping their child together a secret, huh?"

Everyone looked at Mayson as he was back asleep.

"He ain't sleeping!" Joanna said. "Wake up, you old fuckin' fart!"

"Stop it!" Rebecca said. "I *won't* have you disrespecting him!"

"And I won't have him get away with any more years for what him and his son had done to my sister. Today's the day, you fuckin' old, raggedy senile motherfucker! If we're all going back to jail then you're coming with us, you and your son!" Joanna said.

"Sugar," Mayson said while his eyes were still closed.

"Don't you try none of that sugar shit on me, you dirty old-fart fucker!" Joanna said. She looked at Rebecca. "*I just know* you're not fucking this man."

"What we do is none of your business," Rebecca said with her head down.

Joanna pointed the gun at Rebecca. "Everything is my business now, and now it's payback time. If you all wanna get out of here alive then I hope your old senile-ass lover brought his checkbook."

Brittney and Gina looked at each other and smiled.

"His phone is even better because he can easily make transactions with it," Brittney said, as she held it up for them all to see. She looked at it. "Wow, he doesn't have a passcode on it. This is easier than I thought!"

"Are you listening, old man? Or should I say, fossil? Because you're even past the point of being old so fossil is more suitable for your age," Joanna said.

"Stop it!" Rebecca said as tears ran down her eyes.

"How much does he pay you to fuck him?" Joanna asked with a grin.

Mayson smiled with his eyes closed.

"Gina! Could you please tell her to stop asking me these types of questions?" Rebecca pleaded.

"I can't control what she says," Gina replied with a huge grin. "In fact, I'm curious to know the answers myself!"

Brittney and Joanna laughed as they nodded in agreement.

"Today's the day, Big May! Payback time has arrived! It's been 40 years since you and your son have had y'alls freedom for having my sister murdered, and now it's time that someone from her family got what they're owed because of it," Joanna said. She got up in Mayson's face and pointed the gun at him as Rebecca and Ellesse shrieked. "We want a smooth transaction, understand?"

Rebecca looked at Mayson as he was back asleep. "He fell back to sleep. He does this a lot."

"Even when you're fucking him?" Joanna asked.

Gina grinned as Brittney burst into laughter. Ellesse stayed expressionless as she looked at Rebecca as she waited for her to answer.

"I don't understand why you're so interested in what I do with him," Rebecca said. She looked at Mayson and then at Joanna. "Could you please just let him sleep?"

"Not until we get our money," Joanna replied as she still pointed the gun at her. "And none of you are leaving this yacht until we do."

CHAPTER 3

THE LIVESTREAM

"C LAYTON? C AN YOU SEE US? W E'RE LIVE RIGHT NOW," V ERNON asked as he walked alongside of Pete, the social media manager for Missing Persons, as Pete livestreamed what was taking place.

"Yes, Vernon, we can all see it. We're all watching it on the big screen," Clayton confirmed, as everyone sat in the family room.

I sighed as I always felt nervous about livestreams because you never knew what was gonna happen during them, but Clayton and Dray wanted proof that they were on the job in finding Mayson, and we couldn't blame them at all for it. I looked over at Lulu as she held a ball of tissue in her hand as she patted her eyes as Miriam still tried her best to comfort her. Layton was back in my arms, and Stormy was back in Carmella's as Dray and Clayton stood over us while Clayton had his phone glued to his ear as we all watched everything unfold right before our eyes as Vernon and several cops entered the yacht area. I felt that we were watching this happen to someone else. It was just a weird feeling because even the area where all of their yachts were docked, everything just looked so different to me as we were seeing it livestreamed.

"Just to let you all know that this is a private livestream as you

"

requested, Clayton, so that's why I'm able to talk to you like this without you all seeing a live chat going on."

"I appreciate it," Clayton said in a nervous tone.

And we were all very nervous. I didn't even wanna say how nervous I was because we weren't even sure if Mayson was even on the yacht, and we didn't know if Jose and Brock were lying about putting Ellesse down in one of the rooms on his yacht. Vernon and his crew had the task of looking for two people now, not just one.

"Clayton, what's Mayson's number so I can try and call him?" Vernon asked.

Clayton gave him his number.

Brittney looked at Mayson's phone as it rang. "The number is PRIVATE. Should I answer it?"

Everyone looked at Gina as if she was the one who should've decided.

"Go ahead," Gina said.

"Hello?" Brittney said.

"Hello? Who am I speaking to?" Vernon asked.

"Who am *I* speaking to?" Brittney asked in a terse tone.

"Well, I'll tell you who I am if you tell me who you are, because I know for sure this isn't Mayson Royce," Vernon said.

"Damn right it's not Mayson Royce. Mayson Royce can't come to his phone right now," Brittney replied with a grin, as Gina and Joanna grinned back at her. "Would you like to leave a message?"

Rebecca looked at Brittney as she sighed, feeling completely defeated in trying to reason with any of them.

Gina got up and grabbed the phone from her. "Who is this?"

"This is Vernon Baucus from Missing Persons. Who is this? It's clear this is someone different other than who I was first talking to," Vernon replied.

"None of your fuckin' business, Vernon Baucus!" Gina said with a laugh.

Brittney and Joanna laughed as Rebecca and Ellesse sighed and shook their heads. Mayson continued to sit silently with his eyes closed as he drifted in and out of sleep.

"Where is Mayson Royce?" Vernon asked.

"What's it to you?" Gina asked with a grin.

"He has been reported missing by his family and his son Clayton gave me his dad's number, and it's clear there's at least two of you women who have his phone. Who are you? I'm not gonna ask you again."

Joanna took the phone from Gina. "It doesn't matter who we are, what matters is that we see justice get served today. Mayson Royce is never seeing his family again until he gives me what he rightfully owes me and my family!"

Vernon looked confused, then, it hit him. "This is *also* a different voice from the first two. Are you one of the jail escapees from this morning? Who am I talking to?"

Since this was on speaker, Rebecca and Ellesse looked at each other. Rebecca looked at Mayson as he was lightly snoring.

"We only talk money! And Mayson Royce can give it to us, and all you need to give us is a way out of here once we get it, Vernon Baucus!" Joanna said.

Gina and Brittney nodded in agreement.

"Are you all on Mayson Royce's yacht?" Vernon asked, as they cautiously approached his yacht with several cops and SWAT team members along with K9 dogs.

"We're not answering any questions until we get the money to get the fuck out of here!" Joanna informed him. "All Mayson Royce has to do is make that transfer to that bank account of mine and everything's fine!"

"Are you on Mayson Royce's yacht?" Vernon asked again. "And is there anyone else on there with the three of you?"

We all sat at the edge of our seats as Vernon and the rest of the cops stood back and away from Mayson's yacht as they had the place completely surrounded by cops. It was clear that Gina, Brittney, and Joanna were on the yacht and were holding Mayson hostage, and we had yet to find out if anyone else was on there as well, especially Ellesse.

"If those fuckin' bitches hurt my gramps then I'm gonna be the one going to prison!" Dray threatened as his voice shook.

"Stay calm, son," Clayton said as his voice shook just as much as Dray's, as Miriam prayed out loud while still holding Lulu.

I got up with Layton and walked over to Dray and led him to sit down with the rest of us as Clayton went over to Miriam and sat down with her and Lulu as he embraced his mom. We were seeing all of this live right now and knew Mayson was on his yacht with these three women who had escaped from jail, and even though we knew one of them, we had no idea what she was capable of doing. We just didn't know her anymore. We also didn't know if Ellesse was really on there or not because none of them mentioned that she was. It was hard to know what to think and my mind ran with a million thoughts about what was going on inside that yacht as Vernon still talked to them while he had it on speaker for all of us to hear as Pete—who was livestreaming it—had the phone pointing at the yacht which had *Royce II* in full view.

Suddenly, there was commotion on the livestream. Pete panned the phone around in its direction to *Chief running up to Vernon!*

"What's going on, man?! What the fuck is going on?! I got a text saying that my girlfriend is on Mayson Royce's yacht, man! Is she in there? Where is she?!" Chief said in a panic.

"We don't know, Chief. Who told you she was in there?" Vernon asked.

"The text was sent anonymously, man!" Chief said. "What's going on? Who's in there?"

Vernon sighed. "We can't confirm it yet, Chief, but we strongly believe it can be the three female jail escapees."

"GINA IS MY EX-GIRLFRIEND, MAN! She's in there?! For real?!" Chief said as a friend tried to hold him back.

"We don't know if it's them for sure, Chief. It's just that I know I spoke to three different women in there who have Mayson Royce's phone, and they all said they want money from him. I don't think it's a coincidence they ended up here because one says she has some kind of issue with Mayson—but won't say what it is."

Chief shook his head. "What are they still doing in there? Why haven't y'all gone in there to get them yet?"

"We need to take every precaution possible, Chief. We want to be safe," Vernon informed him.

"I'm going down there," Dray said, as he got up.

"NO!" I said, as I pulled him back down. "Let Vernon and the cops do their job, Dray! We are watching everything live right now! They already have Chief who came there when he should've stayed at home or wherever he was since he said he got that text about Ellesse being on there and he doesn't even have proof of it."

"Jose and Brock better not have been lying to me about that," Dray said.

"You just never know, Dray, okay? It's clear that Gina, Brittney, not Joanna mentioned Ellesse being on there with them so we don't know until they get everyone off that yacht."

"There shouldn't be anyone on there right now," Clayton said. "The only one who would be on there around this time would be my dad and his friends, but most of the time it would be just him and only him."

And probably Rebecca, I thought, but I didn't wanna say anything because I didn't wanna cause a mess more than what was already caused.

Auer came back into the room with Todd. We all exchanged formalities.

"Have a seat," Clayton said to him, as he kept his arm around Lulu and his eyes glued to the TV.

"So this is live now?" Todd asked as he sat down in a chair next to the couch Miriam, Clayton, and Lulu were on.

"What the fuck you think, man?!" Dray said.

"Dray!" I said.

"Drayton!" Miriam said.

"My apologies, Mr. Royce. It's just that I wasn't able to see it while Brodwin drove me here since it is a private livestream," Todd said.

I looked at Dray since it was clear he'd forgotten that it was private where we were the only people watching it.

"Well, you're watching it now," Dray said to Todd, and shook his head.

"I'm sorry," I mouthed to Todd, since he wasn't gonna get an apology from Dray. He nodded back with a smile. I looked at the TV and then looked at Todd once again as he stared at me with a smile.

"All right, nap time is over, you limp-dick fucker! I want my fuckin' money for 40 years worth of pain you put me and my family through and I want it right now because I'm tired of waiting because I waited long enough for you to come to your senile senses and it's clear you haven't, but too fuckin' bad now. You robbed me of a lifetime of a relationship I could've had with my older sister, so you're gonna have to come clean about it in the form of money, and I'm gonna try not to be that greedy about it, so I'll take $400 million from your personal account since I know that won't put a dent in it."

Gina laughed. "It really won't put a dent in it at all!"

"And I'll take $47 million, the amount I wanted Angela to give me. Actually, I wanted a lot more than that, but I won't be that greedy this time around," Brittney said.

Joanna pointed the gun at Mayson's head! Rebecca and Ellesse shrieked!

"The sooner you give us this money the better, you fuckin' fossil fucker, you hear?" Joanna said.

Mayson slowly opened his eyes. "Lulu?"

"Not this fuckin' shit again!" Brittney said as she shook her head.

"I'll be anyone you want me to be as soon as I get my money!" Joanna said.

"Lulu?" Mayson said again.

Joanna pointed the gun at Rebecca! "Make him stop saying this shit right now!"

"I can't control what he says! I told you he's senile! He doesn't know what he is saying more than half of the time!" Rebecca said as tears streamed from her eyes as she held her hands up in the air.

Mayson slowly slumped over on his right side!

"Oh, my goodness!" Ellesse said.

Mayson slowly lifted a gun towards Gina, Brittney, and Joanna! "If you bitches don't get the *FUCK* off my boat!"

They screamed as Joanna dropped Mayson's phone and ran as fast as they could out of the room as Ellesse ran with them!

"STOP! POLICE!" Vernon and the other cops yelled as they all ran off the yacht!

"ELLESSE!!!" Chief yelled.

"CHIEF!" Ellesse yelled back.

"Chief?! Who the fuck is he to you?" Gina asked.

"My boyfriend!" Ellesse said.

"Your *boyfriend*?! Your motherfuckin' *boyfriend*? And you're pregnant by *Dray*?" Gina asked Ellesse, and pulled out her gun!

"DROP YOUR WEAPON!" the cops yelled.

"YOU TRIFLIN'-ASS TRICK!" Gina said, and fired two shots at Ellesse, killing her instantly.

"NOOOOOOOOO! GINA!!!!!" Chief yelled as he was being held back by cops and friends. "ELLESSE!!!!!"

"DROP YOUR WEAPON! DROP YOUR WEAPON!" the cops yelled as Gina held it down by her side . . . and pointed it towards them . . . and was lit up with a barrage of bullets!

Joanna screamed as she pulled out her gun towards the cops and got off a few shots . . . and was met with the same fate as Gina.

"Don't shoot! Don't shoot! Stop shooting! Stop shooting!" Brittney screamed as she laid on the ground completely covering her head.

And just as fast as it started, it had ended.

Vernon, as well as some of the cops, came over to all of them to check if they were still alive. Female cops came over to Brittney, cuffed her, and helped her to her feet as they led her away for questioning.

Three dead, one injured.

Several minutes later, a female cop escorted Rebecca off of the yacht, and two male cops escorted Mayson off right behind her while the rest of the cops searched for other possible people inside the yacht. They sat in separate cop cars as they were questioned.

We all sat in a stunned silence with what we'd witnessed live right in front of our eyes. I was so glad this livestream was private. With all of the things we'd been through, this was the toughest to watch three people be killed on live TV. The best thing that'd happened was that Mayson was not one of them, and Vernon had told us he was going to be checked out by paramedics and then was cleared to come home as soon as he was. We were just waiting on the call.

"So they weren't lying to me," Dray said, in terms of what Brock and Jose had told him about putting Ellesse in Mayson's yacht, only to have her killed by Gina once they were right outside of it. Everyone acted as if they didn't wanna address the elephant in the room, and that was that Dray was the cause of this happening to begin with. "I know Chief is really fucked up right now. His ex-girlfriend killed his current girlfriend, and he witnessed it all just several feet in front of him. Damn."

No one said a word. I think we were all still too shocked and stunned at what we'd all witnessed, and it would be etched in our minds forever just like all of the rest of the fucked-up shit we'd been through.

Clayton's phone rang. "Clayton Royce."

"Hey, Clayton, it's Vernon. I'm sorry again for what you all had to witness on that livestream. That's why I asked you were you all sure that you wanted to watch it live because anything could've happened, and it did."

"Yeah, man, that was way worse than what we ever thought was gonna happen. We've been through some shit in this family, but seeing something like that as it happened was just awful, man, just awful. But how is my dad? Is he on his way back here?"

"He is, Clayton. That's what I was calling you about. He answered as many questions as he could, but he seemed a little incoherent at times. His female friend Rebecca was able to fill us in about what went on in the yacht, as well as Brittney Hart."

"Thanks for all of your help, Vernon."

CHAPTER 4

THE BLOCK

A SEA OF MEDIA STOOD IN GREAT ANTICIPATION AT THE END OF OUR driveway waiting to hear what we had to say in terms of what'd happened earlier at Mayson's yacht, as well as people wanting to hear from the Royce patriarch himself about his ordeal with coming face-to-face with three female jail escapees with now two of them being dead along with Ellesse who was held in there since she herself went "missing."

Todd stood up at the podium while we all stood behind him. Clayton had his arm around Mayson as Lulu held Mayson's hand with her right hand. I stood next to Dray as I held Layton and he held Stormy. Miriam stood next to Clayton on his right side. The sky once again had an ominous cast that completely covered it, making it appear as if it was going to rain in a second. Our bodyguards surrounded us as well as some stood by the media.

Todd looked over his notes and got ready to speak. "Thank you all for being here this afternoon for this press conference over the incident involving Royce patriarch Mayson Royce and what had occurred outside of his yacht. This has been a very difficult incident to process since you know, three people lost their lives during it, with two being jail escapees Gina Knight and Joanna Woodburn. The third person killed was Ellesse Rosati, who we believe was being held hostage by the three women, and who was also reported missing a while back. We still don't know how she ended up in Mayson's yacht."

I tried not to side-eye Dray as I'm sure he tried not to side-eye me. I knew there was going to be a lot of questions as to how Ellesse ended up in there, and we were all under a strict order not to talk about it, especially now since Ellesse was dead.

"Mayson Royce, as you all can see, is alive and well. We don't know the exact details of everything that had happened this morning into this afternoon, and we will not be speculating on it. We will also not be answering any questions about this matter. Thank you," Todd said.

Pictures began flashing like crazy as we all turned around and headed back into the house as the reporters still shouted their questions at us as the wrought iron gates closed in front of them.

Several minutes later, Mayson sat on the couch with Lulu as we all wanted to hear from him about what'd really happened.

"I was coherent the whole time. I made those women believe I was senile, and they believed it. Boy, they called me all kinds of old fucks and everything, but I knew I had to keep playing the kind of person they thought I was," Mayson said in his raspy voice.

"We were so worried about you, Dad. We heard about them escaping very early in their escape, and when I couldn't get in touch with you, I knew something was seriously wrong. What happened to your phone?" Clayton asked.

"I didn't have it turned on. I turned it off and thought I still had it on. Sorry I scared the shit out of all of you. You know I didn't mean to."

"You're forgiven," Dray said with a smile.

Everyone nodded in agreement.

"Was that young lady really on my boat for all of that time she was reported missing?" Mayson asked Dray.

Everyone looked at him.

"That's what they told me, Gramps," Dray replied.

"Why the hell did they put her in *my* boat? Why couldn't they have put her in yours?" Mayson asked.

Everyone looked in different directions.

"I don't know why they did what they did and why she was even in there. It doesn't matter anymore because they've been let go. Both of them," Dray informed him.

I gasped as I looked at him. "What?!"

"I said what I said, Eve. I don't wanna talk about it," Dray said.

"I understand," I replied. But he knew damn well I wanted to talk about this later since they were some of the bodyguards that'd been with him for years. I looked at Leon and Auer as they both stared back at me, and I knew they definitely wanted to talk about it. I also knew there was way more to the story as to what went on in that yacht.

"Well, I didn't wanna say this in front of everyone, but Rebecca is the one who really kept me alive in there, as well as herself, as well as that young girl Ellesse, until she ran out of there," Mayson said, as him, Clayton, and Dray sat in Dray's mancave.

"I knew there was more to this story, Gramps. I knew that out of respect, Vernon didn't wanna say that Rebecca is your mistress and of course Todd knew not to even mention her name at the press conference either," Dray said.

"And I appreciate it, but I just don't know if I would still be here if it wasn't for her. My number two really came through for me," Mayson said as he shook his head. He sighed. "That Joanna just couldn't let the past go, and now she's right along with her sister."

"She brought it up, huh?" Clayton asked, and took a sip of his drink.

"Like it happened yesterday," Mayson said.

"She has no proof of anything," Dray said. "I know I wasn't even born yet when her sister was murdered, but I know you all had nothing to do with it. That woman just wanted money back then for a child she couldn't prove was yours, Dad."

"And her sister wanted $400 million from me today," Mayson said.

"Doesn't surprise me," Clayton said.

"Me neither," Dray said.

"That little Brittney chick tried to get $47 million out of me claiming she wanted one of the payments her mom was supposed to get from you, Dray," Mayson said. "I had enough of their bullshit and pretended to slump over dead, and that's when I grabbed my gun out of the drawer on the side of the couch I was sitting on and pointed it at them; sent all of those bitches running out of there! Joanna even dropped my phone before she ran, but I don't know why that Ellesse girl ran with them. I was actually trying to protect her."

"She was probably just shocked and confused since she'd been in there for so long and finally saw her chance to get out of there as well," Dray said. "Sorry she was put in there, Gramps. I don't know why they did that. It made it look like you had something to do with her disappearance which in turn made the whole Royce family look like we did."

"Was it your child she was pregnant with?" Clayton asked.

Mayson looked at him.

Dray shook his head and then shrugged his shoulders. "It's possible."

"Because if they find out that it was then we're in trouble with Chief as a client, son. Everyone heard Gina say that Ellesse said she was pregnant with your child, but she was Chief's girlfriend," Clayton said.

"Gina was fucked up, Dad. You know that. She just completely lost it when she got involved with you."

"This isn't about me, Dray, and you know it!"

"Settle down, you two," Mayson warned. "You know what kind of day I had."

"And it was hard on everyone in this family, Dad," Clayton reminded him.

"Well, I'm still here," Mayson said.

"You had multiple affairs with Gina while she was with Chief and it didn't affect his status as a client of ours," Dray said.

"I didn't get her pregnant either, Dray!" Clayton said. "You know after what Eve did at his restaurant, he was about to end his relationship as a personal client with us and was definitely gonna invest his restaurant with some other company."

"And I talked him out of it, remember?" Dray said.

"And how are you gonna talk him out of the fact that you got his now-dead girlfriend pregnant?" Clayton asked. "He probably thought that baby was his! A baby she will never have now!"

"I did it before with talking with him and I will do it again," Dray replied.

"This is different, Dray! This girl is dead! Both of those girls are dead that he was involved with! But one was pregnant and she was pregnant by you!"

"Why are you taking a dead girl's side, Dad?"

Mayson looked at Clayton.

"This isn't about taking sides, Dray, this is about business. You got that girl pregnant, caused her to become missing because of your bodyguards putting her in your grandfather's yacht because they thought they were doing you a favor, and now she's dead because she was pregnant by you and not by Chief, and in Gina's convoluted mind she thought she was still Chief's girlfriend."

"I think she still would've shot Ellesse if it was Chief's child. You even said the bitch was fucked up and she was."

"Doesn't matter, Dray. You were the cause of all of this and you know it. You getting that girl pregnant put everything in motion. That girl is dead because of you."

"Now, Clayton, don't go saying shit like that. It's not Dray's fault."

"It's not. And if I'm the cause of Ellesse's death then who is the cause of Jolene Woodburn's death? Huh?"

Clayton raised his hand at Dray, but Mayson blocked his attempt to hit him!

Tears welled up in Dray's eyes.

"Don't you ever mention her again. *Ever*," Clayton said, and stormed off.

Dray turned and looked at Mayson.

"You heard him, grandson," Mayson said, and left as well.

CHAPTER 5
THE WRONGDOINGS

<u>HOT COFFEE, TEA, AND JUST ME</u>
BREAKING NEWS!
WHEN YACHTING AND THOTTING GOES VERY
WRONG!
3 DEAD AT MAYSON ROYCE'S YACHT
CAUSES OF DEATHS: DRAY ROYCE AND FAMILY!

"Yeah, and I said what I said! Welcome back to my show, every-one, I'm Nika Rose, the only one you'll ever need for all of your epic hot coffee and tea, and I got it all right here as I always do! Yeah, I am back after a brief hiatus and let's just put it out there —y'all know who was the cause of it! His name is in the title, but his whore wife's name should be in it as well because I know she was the one who put him up to it because he's the one with all of the power, not her. But neither one of them had that much power to keep me away because I was not gonna be silenced forever so here I am, and I am back with a vengeance in this latest that was clearly caused by no other than Dray Royce! And he dragged is philandering grandfather Mayson and slut mistress Rebecca into all of this as well.

"So, here's what's been confirmed. Three are dead, and they are Gina Knight, former girlfriend of baseball star Chief Smith; Ellesse Rosati, current girlfriend of Chief Smith and confirmed pregnant by Chief and her family; and Joanna Woodburn, who I was told by a reliable source has a past connection with the Royce family by way of her late sister Jolene Woodburn, who was murdered 40 years ago and whose killer has not been found to this day. And yes, you heard me say that there is a past connection with the Royce family and it has everything to do with Joanna's sister Jolene, so I think you all know what I could be getting at."

She picked up her teapot and poured tea into her teacup and took a slow sip. She put the teacup down as she shook her head while she looked at her computer.

"Damn. And because there is a past connection, my source told me that people had spoken directly to Rebecca, who everyone knows is Mayson Royce's mistress, and she said that Joanna brandished a gun at Mayson inside the yacht demanding money from him because of her sister's death. Brittney Hart, the oldest daughter of the late Angela Hart and the mother of Stormy, Dray Royce's daughter, demanded $47 million from him since she couldn't get it from her mom and killed her as a result of it. Gina was reported to have wanted nothing from him; she just didn't wanna go back to jail and eventually to prison for the murders she committed, and just wanted a way out of town which is what they all wanted after they got money them bitches knew damn well they weren't gonna get. I honestly don't know how they all got off the boat, but my source told me that Rebecca had gotten a gun somehow and scared them off, but Ellesse ran with them when she was trying to protect her."

"That's not what happened. The bitch is lying," Dray said as he shook his head as we watched this while in bed.

"I believe you when you said your gramps told you and your dad that he had the gun and scared them out of his yacht. Maybe that's what Rebecca told the cops was that she had the gun instead of your gramps?"

"I don't know what she told them. But it was clear Gramps didn't say anything to the cops about pointing a gun at all of them, and he didn't say Rebecca had a gun either. I wish I could get this bitch silenced again because she's talking about shit her ass shouldn't be talking about and it's gonna get her in trouble."

I looked at him. "Dray, now don't go making threats, okay? You knew the gag order on her wasn't gonna last forever, and she was gonna be right back to doing what she's doing; the surprise would've been if she didn't. I don't even know why they even have those things if they can't be permanent."

"Because they know they're useless being permanent, Eve. The only way someone's gag order will be permanent is if they're silenced for good."

"I know, and I don't want you getting any ideas. This is over, honey, okay? We have our family patriarch back, no one ever has to worry about Gina killing anyone else ever again, or Joanna asking for money she doesn't deserve," I said. But didn't know how I felt about Joanna not deserving anything at all after what Floyd had told me. I just didn't wanna start an argument. "The only one I feel sorry for in this case is Ellesse, and I know it's surprising for me to say that, but she didn't deserve to be murdered. What's gonna happen with her?"

He shrugged. "I honestly don't know, Eve. My lawyers are already telling me something I've heard a million times—don't be surprised if I'm sued by her family. But there's no reason in the world I should be sued by them. There is no proof I had anything to do with this or that the baby she was carrying was really mine."

"But it's possible that it is yours, Dray. And she was killed by Gina because of it. Gina just became really fucked up after she started screwing around with your dad."

"Watch it," he warned.

"What?! Watch *what*, Dray? What?! Don't tell me you're gonna sit here and say that all of what had happened today didn't start with the two of you?"

"FUCK YOU!" he said, and jumped out of bed!

I gasped as tears welled up in my eyes as I shook my head. I turned the video back on because I had to hear what else this bitch had to say:

"And that private livestream—the one that hasn't been leaked yet since it was streamed by the police department—said that Gina popped Ellesse because she was Chief's girlfriend but admitted that she was pregnant by Dray. And Chief saw both of those bitches get blasted live in front of his eyes! Yeah, Dray Royce seems to be the common denominator in everything; the cause of everything. And my source told me that Chief is inconsolable about what he witnessed and when asked about Dray, he said nothing at all as he was led away by cops and his friends. Stay tuned for this one because this hot-ass mess is far from over!"

I got out of bed and went to look for Dray . . . and found him in the bathroom of his office. "Dray?"

He emerged from it as he walked past me with bloodshot eyes. I knew he was crying.

I grabbed his arm. "Dray, what's wrong? I know you're not crying about what Nika was saying."

"Fuck no," he said as he wiped his eyes with his only free hand.

I led him over to one of his couches, and was surprised he actually sat next to me.

He sighed. "He raised his hand at me."

"Who raised their hand at you, Dray?"

"My dad. He hasn't done that shit to me since I was a teen and in my twenties."

"Why did he do it?"

He sighed as he shook his head. "I said something I should not have said; brought up some shit I shouldn't have brought up. And it was all because of what happened today."

"Where do I start with that?"

"Please, Eve."

"Dray, I'm not trying to be funny. It's clear your dad really hurt you by raising his hand at you as if he was gonna hit you. It would hurt anyone who's close to a parent and they do that. But even though he didn't do it, I know it hurt you to see how he was about to."

"It always does, Eve. It's just that I'm tired of being the cause of everything, but when I bring up something that he was the cause of, he wants to keep it buried as if it never happened."

I started to get a sickening feeling. "What did your dad cause and what does it have to do with what happened today?" I wanted him to tell me what Floyd had told me.

He sighed. "It doesn't matter anymore, Eve. What's done is done."

"If it didn't matter so much then why are you so upset about it? Something happened earlier between you and your dad and it had something to do with what'd happened today. I think you'll feel a lot better if you tell me, Dray. You know I'm not gonna say anything."

He shook his head. "Forget it, Eve." He got up.

I pulled him back down. "I'm not forgetting anything, Dray. There is no way we're gonna be able to forget what'd happened today."

"And I'm more worried about Chief than anything."

"I think you need to talk to Chief, Dray. The sooner the better. It's all out in the open now. He knows Ellesse was pregnant with your child. Avoiding any contact with him is just gonna make things worse. The sooner the two of you sit down and talk, the better. There's nothing anyone can do for Ellesse, her baby, and Gina—but I know Chief expects to hear from you, Dray. Not talking to him makes you look bad."

"I don't wanna lose him as a client or a friend, Eve."

"And that's exactly why the two of you need to talk about this. This is just something that can't be avoided. Ellesse was put in your grandfather's yacht by your now-former bodyguards; she was pregnant with your baby. Chief wants the answers that Ellesse can't give him, I know he does."

"I just don't know what to say to him."

"Say that you were wrong, that's the first thing. There has been so many wrongdoings in what happened today that we need to start making things right. Chief witnessed these killings of two women he was involved with; it doesn't get any more fucked up than that. You need to do this, Dray."

Auer appeared at the door. "Dray?"

Dray looked up. "What is it, man?"

"I just got word from the front entrance that Chief is here to see you."

I looked at Dray.

Dray sighed. "Let him in."

CHAPTER 6

THE FACE-OFF

"I WANT THE TWO OF YOU TO STAY RIGHT OUTSIDE OF THESE DOORS," I told Leon, as we stood outside of Dray's office. "I just don't know how this is gonna go."

"We'll do whatever you want us to do. You know we got y'all," Leon assured me while speaking for Auer.

I knew he did, but I was extremely nervous. I hadn't been this nervous since I was over at Chief's house for a night with him that I didn't wanna have with him. Now he was coming over here since everything was out in the open now about Dray really getting Ellesse pregnant, and even though she was no longer here, I felt Dray and Chief needed to talk about this face-to-face, man-to-man.

I looked to my left and saw Auer and Chief walk up the right side of the double wrought-iron staircase. I immediately tensed up. They seemed as if they were a mile down this extremely wide hallway, and it seemed as if it was taking them forever to reach us. I locked eyes with Chief; he didn't look happy at all as expected. After witnessing two women that he had relationships with get murdered, I didn't expect anything more from him right now. I just wanted him and Dray to try and talk this out.

Chief and Auer approached us.

"Hello, Chief," I said in a somber tone. I just felt so awkward talking to him.

"Eve, Leon," Chief said with a nod, and the dismal tone in his voice said everything.

"I'm so sorry for your loss," I said. I stepped towards him to give him a hug.

He barely hugged me back. "Where's Dray?"

"In his office. You can go on in," I replied as I tried to smile, but failed miserably.

Chief nodded as he looked in Dray's office. He then looked at me. "I want you in here, too. I want you both to hear what I have to say."

This didn't sound good at all.

"Okay," I replied in a cracked voice. I let him walk in ahead of me.

Dray stood in front of his desk as he stared at me, and then stared at Chief. "Chief. How are you holding up, man?"

"Not well," Chief replied as he gave Dray a look I'd never seen him give him before. I'd never seen him this upset while he was in our presence, but he had a million reasons to be the way he was right now, so I didn't blame him one bit.

"I'd like to extend to you my deepest condolences on your loss today," Dray said, and extended his hand out for a shake.

Chief sighed as he stared up at the ceiling. His hands didn't budge by his side. "You should be extending your condolences to me for a lot of things, man, a lot of things."

I looked at Dray. This was more serious than I thought it was. I looked back to see if Leon and Auer were still right outside the door, and they stood right outside of it as if they were ready to run in here, and it also appeared as if they were blocking Chief from leaving.

Dray sighed as he looked down at the floor. "Chief. Look, man. I fucked up with a lot of shit, a lot of shit."

"And you fucked my girl, man? Was she really pregnant by you? Yes or no?"

I once again looked at Dray. I really wanted to know how he was going to answer this.

"I'm sorry, man," Dray replied as he still looked at the ground.

Chief let out a sigh and shook his head. "Sorry? *SORRY*?! Naw, man. The last thing you are is sorry. Did you have someone put my girl in the bottom of your grandfather's yacht?"

"Absolutely not, Chief!" Dray said.

"Chief, he's not lying about that," I confirmed to him.

"Then how the hell did she get down there?" Chief asked.

"My former bodyguards did that—and as you heard I said former because they no longer work for me. I had nothing to do with any of that. Nothing. Yes, man, I did have sex with Ellesse, and I was wrong for it just as much as she was. For some reason, my bodyguards wanted to put her in my grandfather's yacht, thinking that they were helping me out or whatever, I don't know."

"Helping you out with what, man? What you're saying doesn't make any sense."

"None of it makes any sense, man. I had nothing to do with her being missing or anything," Dray said.

"And now she's dead. Dead along with Gina. I hated Gina after what she did to that girl at y'alls penthouse, and then she kills someone else while in jail and now she killed my current pregnant girlfriend who said she was pregnant by you, man! *YOU!* I heard it with my own fuckin' ears, man!"

"Chief, please stay calm. Our son is in his room sleeping," I informed him, even though Layton's room seemed like it was a mile from here.

"Why, man? Why my girl, huh? Because you let me have sex with Eve to sign my business as a client?" Chief asked. "Do you always have to get every girl you want even though you're married?"

"I don't wanna talk about that," I warned him. "What's done is done with it."

"It's relevant, Eve," Chief said.

"No it's not," Dray said.

"THE HELL IT ISN'T, MOTHERFUCKER!!" Chief yelled.

Auer and Leon took more steps into the office.

"My wife asked you to stay calm, Chief. You came over here to talk to me and I'm talking to you. We're not gonna get anywhere with you yelling like this," Dray said.

Chief shook his head. "I thought you were my friend, man. One of my best friends," he said in a cracked voice as I saw tears welling up in his eyes. "You are the cause of all of this shit, man, and you know it! You know it!"

"I'm sorry, man, I really am," Dray said as well in a cracked voice.

And I didn't think he was trying to make Chief feel sorry for him, I think he really meant it. I also thought this was the very first time he was faced with having to tell the truth to a friend about fucking their girlfriend, but he took it to a whole other level by getting her pregnant, and even though Ellesse wasn't here anymore, it didn't change the facts in this situation at all.

"You have everything, man! *Everything!* You have all the money, a beautiful wife and kids, looks, status, and power that you want! Why are you always causing bad shit to happen? *Why?*"

"Because I'm not perfect, man. I'm a fuckup. No one knows how bad I feel about everything bad that I've caused."

Chief shook his head. "Too bad, man. Too bad."

"What do you mean?" Dray asked.

"It's too late, man. It's too bad, man. I just can't with this anymore with you. I just can't, man. I've been through too much shit, man, too much. This is it . . . I just—"

I screamed as Chief came charging towards Dray!

Auer and Leon tackled him to the ground as Dray jumped out of the way!

"I HATE YOU, MAN! I HATE YOU! FUCK YOU, DRAY ROYCE! WE'RE NO LONGER FRIENDS! I'M NO LONGER A CLIENT OF ROYCE INVESTMENTS—BUSINESS AND PERSONAL! HAVE MY SHIT TRANSFERRED TO GILCREST INVESTMENTS! AND I FUCKIN' MEAN IT, MOTHER-FUCKER! FUCK YOU AND THE ROYCE FAMILY!" Chief yelled as Auer and Leon picked him up off the floor and led him out the room.

Tears streamed down my eyes as I stood in the corner of Dray's office as Chief continued to yell and rant about now hating him and therefore hating us and everything about us until his voice completely faded out in the distance, and this was all caused by Dray.

"I don't want wanna talk about it. I wanna be alone," he said as he stared down at the floor.

I cried as I walked out of his office. I was not gonna argue with him.

CHAPTER 7

THE TRANSFER

THERE WAS A KNOCK ON DRAY'S DOOR AT HIS OFFICE AT WORK.

"Come in!" Dray said, as he sat working on his computer at his desk.

Clayton walked in! "Hey, son."

"Hey," Dray said as he continued to work on his computer without looking at him.

Clayton walked towards him. "You got a few minutes?"

"Not really," Dray replied.

Clayton sat down in front of his desk. "Son, look. I'm sorry about what I did the last time we saw each other."

"It's done, Dad, okay? I don't wanna talk about it. We lost a huge client so that's my main focus right now."

"Who?" Clayton asked with curiosity piqued all in his voice.

"Chief," Dray replied as he still tended to his computer.

"You're kidding, Dray," he said as he shook his head.

"Unfortunately, I'm not. I'm actually surprised you didn't hear. I thought you came in here to talk to me about it."

Clayton sighed as he shook his head. "What happened?"

"Well, everyone who was watching the livestream that day at Gramps's yacht knows what happened."

42

Clayton sighed once again. "This is why you know you should not have done what you did with that girl, son. Even though she's dead, it's clear Chief has not let this go, and now it has cost us him as a client—business and personal."

"What's done is done, right? I can't take back anything that I caused. He came charging at me like a one-percenter Rottweiler at my home last night in front of Eve and our bodyguards. He had every right to be as upset as he is. He said he hated me and didn't wanna be a client here anymore. I'm having my assistants working right now on getting his stuff transferred to Gilcrest."

"Doesn't he want to think this over more first? It's a pretty hasty decision to make right away. I just don't think they can do for him like the way we have been and always will be able to do. We're pretty much responsible for making him the richest man in sports."

"That's what he wants, Dad. I can't stop him from leaving. It's my fault that he is. I take full responsibility. He may be a big client of ours, but he's not the biggest. We're gonna lose a lot of money with him no longer being with us, but we're not gonna lose a fortune. I just have to deal with the consequences of my actions. Like you, Eve, Chief, and everyone else said, I'm the cause of this so I'm being the man I am and dealing with it."

"Very well, son," he said. He got up. "If you wanna talk about this some more, I'll be in my office."

Dray nodded as he still worked on his computer. He looked at a framed picture of him and Chief at one of his biggest games from a few years back. He sighed as he shook his head and continued to work.

"I'm glad you decided to have lunch with me, Eve. I really need you here right now," Dray said, as we ate lunch in the suite area of his office.

"You know I'm always gonna be here for you, Dray. I just wanna know how it's been going for you today. I'm actually surprised you wanted to come into work today after everything that'd happened yesterday."

"Besides you and my kids, it's the only thing that's keeping me sane right now."

"Well, I'm glad to hear that," I replied with a smile. I sighed. "So, it's really happening?"

"Yeah, it is. My assistants are still working on Chief's transfer. There's nothing I can do about it. He has not called me to personally stop it from happening so it's clear he wants to go through with it. My dad even thought I was kidding at first when I told him he didn't wanna be a client anymore—business or personal. This is when I truly regret doing what I did, Eve. We lost a big client just because I slept with his girlfriend."

"And just to think I slept with him to get him as a business client of ours because of what I did at his business. This shit has just got to stop, Dray. There's always a better way, but it starts with you being a better person; with all of us being better people."

"Can't argue with that, Eve. That's why you're the best. You won't stop at anything to tell me exactly what I need to hear."

"I can tell you everything you need to hear, Dray, but you need to put in the work to make yourself that everything I tell you that you need to hear. Of course none of us are perfect; we all need to work on something. But when something like this happens with you doing something so personal and it affected a good friend of yours and we lose him as a friend and a client and he was no ordinary client, then this is serious, Dray. We don't want this to happen again."

"It's not gonna happen again, Eve. I'm sure of it."

"I hope not, Dray. But do you really believe Chief hates you?"

He sighed. "Yeah, I really think he does. There is never gonna be a completely cooling-off period for him. Like I told my dad, he charged at me like a one-percenter Rottweiler; you saw it with your own eyes."

"Yeah, I saw it all right."

"I could see all of the rage in his eyes. He'd never done that shit to me before. If it wasn't for Auer and Leon getting to him so fast and tackling him to the ground, I believe he would've beat the shit out of me and I would've deserved every bit of it."

"Well, that's what we have them for. They could sense the trouble just as much as I could."

"It seems like everyone wants to beat my ass and rightfully so. At least my dad tried to apologize for almost ready to do it."

"And almost doesn't count because he didn't do it, Dray. Like I said, you really need to work on being a better person when it comes to your personal life. And as I said before, I'm not just singling you out, I'm talking about myself as well because everyone has something they need to work on. When your personal life starts messing with your professional life, then that's a problem—a big problem—because it's messing with our livelihood."

"You're right, Eve. Our livelihood is everything."

We were interrupted by Breaking News on the local TV news:

"We just received some Breaking News. An early-morning jogger discovered a black Rolls-Royce Phantom in a ditch just off of Sapphire Valley Road. When he checked to see if there was anyone inside the car, he made a shocking discovery to it being baseball star Chief Smith, currently the richest man in sports. We have no idea of his condition so we will keep you all updated as soon as new information becomes available."

Dray immediately got on his phone.

"Who are you calling?"

"CHIEF!" he yelled as he stood up and walked around the area.

"Dray . . ."

"Eve, please! Okay? I don't care how much he hates me. I wanna see how he is. I don't even know how long he could've been in that ditch. He left our house in a fit of fury last night and rightfully so, and no one knew where he was all night? He was discovered by an early morning jogger? I gotta know how he is, Eve. He may hate me, and I don't blame him, but I still consider him my friend."

My eyes welled up with tears as I nodded in agreement. I didn't know how this was gonna turn out, but I also wanted to hear how he was because this didn't sound good at all. I just wanted him to be okay.

"Dray."

We looked around as Clayton stood before us.

He came over to Dray and embraced him. Dray broke down and cried.

I managed to crack a smile as tears streamed down from my eyes. I knew he'd heard about Chief as well, but I knew this was also about the fight they'd gotten into with each other before what'd happened to Chief. I was happy at this point to see some forgiveness from someone.

CHAPTER 8

THE CONDITIONS

<u>HOT COFFEE, TEA, AND JUST ME</u>
BREAKING NEWS!
BASEBALL STAR CHIEF SMITH IN CRITICAL
CONDITION
THE RICHEST MAN IN SPORTS WAS FOUND UNRE-
SPONSIVE INSIDE ROLLS-ROYCE IN A DITCH

"And I really hate to say this, but who didn't see this coming? This man has been through some shit for real! And now he may be just as gone as his current girlfriend Ellesse and his ex-girlfriend Gina because of it. Hello, everyone, and welcome to the show, I'm Nika Rose, the only one you'll ever need for all of your epic hot coffee and tea, and I knew there was a reason why I was brought back to doing videos at this time because there is a lot that has been going down lately and it is all because of the Royce family."

She picked up her teapot and poured tea into it, and then picked up the coffee pot and poured coffee into her coffee mug.

47

"I have to double fist on the caffeine tonight because both pots are steaming hot! And you know I don't do this too often, but I do it when there's just too much shit going on and it all comes back to the Royces, particularly, Dray. Now my sources have been gathering information all day about Chief since the news broke about him, and one told me in particular that he was coming from Dray's house when he got into this so-called accident that landed him in a ditch. And the reason why I say so-called is because when anything involves the Royce family, you have to look at everything. Everything. I believe a hundred percent that Chief was coming from Dray's house because he had every right to confront him about getting his now-dead girlfriend Ellesse pregnant. And just remember, Gina, his ex-girlfriend, was having an affair with Clayton Royce. It was like she got all fucked up after being involved with him even though she was currently Chief's girlfriend at the time and even went to Dray and Eve's fake wedding with him. Honestly, for the life of me, I just don't understand why these women wanna fuck around with the Royce men when all it does is get them pregnant, in trouble, or dead—or all three. Yeah, just ask Angela Hart, Dray's baby mama about that—oh, sorry, you can't, and everyone knows why. To this day, I'll always believe he had something to do with her death and put her oldest daughter Brittney up to doing it. And ironically, Brittney is the only who came out alive at that old fossil's yacht that day out of the three jail escapees. Very interesting."

"This bitch really needs to shut the fuck up because I had nothing to do with Angela's death, and that was proven. I never knew Brittney existed just like everyone else didn't know until she confessed to the cops," Dray said, as we sat with Layton and Stormy in the recreation room.

"Dray, I know you didn't. But what I do believe is that she really does believe that you did put Brittney up to it. She just can't let it go. There's nothing anyone can do for Angela now." I looked at Stormy as

Dray held her. I still felt so sorry for her and I always would that she had no idea her mom was dead and that her older sister had killed her.

"And what is she trying to say about Chief? It sounds to me that he was in an unfortunate accident. He was mad when he left here."

"Yeah, he was. That's why I wish someone would've drove him here and back home. Well, let's find out because she's not gonna stop running her big, fat fuckin' mouth about it," I said, as we continued to watch:

"My source got some viable information about why and how
Chief ended up in his car in a ditch because he was in fact over
at Dray's house to confront him about getting Ellesse pregnant,
and it was said that Dray denied it, of course, but got pissed off
at Chief for even implying that he would do something like
that. But what Dray got pissed off more about was that Chief
ended their friendship and him being a client at Royce Investments—business *and* personal."

I looked at Dray. "How did she find out about this? This part is accurate, Dray."

He sighed as he shook his head. "I know it is, Eve. But I know Auer and Leon didn't say anything because they were the only ones who witnessed what'd happened in my office with Chief, as well as you."

We continued to watch:

She took a sip of her tea, and then took a sip of her coffee.
"Told you why I needed to double fist on the caffeine tonight!
And everyone knows that Dray has been the cause of everything. I believe Dray had his bodyguards beat Chief up more
for wanting to terminate his client relationship with him
because business to Dray is more important than friendship and
family."

"Don't you believe that for a second, Eve. This bitch is clearly starting shit like she always does. I believe all of these things are of equal importance."

"I know you do, Dray. But when she has a story about us, she always likes to embellish shit about it. I wish we could get her removed from social media and online for good."

"We tried, Eve. She's just gonna keep coming back because she has nothing going on in her life of any importance that's why she does what she does. She's a dime-a-dozen wannabe famous bitch by way of talking shit about people she will never be like; about people she wishes she lived like. But she's crossed the line way too many times."

"And she's not worth you getting into any real trouble over, Dray."

"She's saying that I'm the cause of everything, Eve. Yeah, I may be the cause of some things, but not everything. I didn't make Gina kill Ellesse because she told her she was pregnant with my baby, she did that on her own, and she ended up lit up by those cops like she should've known she was gonna be and she should've been. Like Joanna, same thing. They knew what they were doing and got what they deserved. I'm just glad my gramps came out of all of this okay."

I smiled. "Me too."

We listened to more of what she had to say:

"Look, Chief is in the condition he's in because he's been
involved with Dray and his family. No one ever ends up in a
better condition than what they started in once they get
involved with Dray and the Royce family. Everyone thinks just
because they're the richest Black family in the world that
they're the most desirable to be around and being around them
will make their lives better. No, it's the opposite, and Chief is
the latest one to attest to that now. His condition may not
improve for him to be able to tell his story, and it's all his fault.
I believe he was ran off the road by Dray and Eve's bodyguards,
Auer and Leon, because they'll do anything for them—especially Leon for Eve. Or, could they have drugged him and one of
his bodyguards put his car in the ditch and him in the driver's
seat? So many possibilities! Stay tuned!"

"We both know damn well Chief left here by himself. Auer and Leon made sure he left."

I sighed. "I didn't see him leave, Dray. And I have to admit to you that I didn't see Auer and Leon after they took Chief out of your office. Did you?"

CHAPTER 9

THE MOOD

"THAT'S IT, BIG TEDDY. KEEP YOUR BIG, HARD FAT FUCKIN' COCK IN my big, hot fat fuckin' cunt! Fuck yeah!" Carmella said, as Auer went fast and hard inside of her.

"Fat, fat, fat," he said as he was out of breath, but was still trying to satisfy her as well as himself.

"Well, I'm not in denial about how I look. I don't know about you."

"I've never been small in height or width," he replied with a grin.

"Me neither!"

They laughed as he pulled out of her and laid right next to her.

"Why did you stop? My pussy's still wetter than a rainstorm. That shit felt fuckin' good, and I needed that."

He grinned. "We both did, Carmella. Especially me."

"Well, we both work for Dray. The way he causes shit puts anyone in the mood to wanna fuck the stress out of them all day, every day."

"It's what we signed up for," he said, as he looked up at the ceiling.

"Yeah, don't remind me," she said, as she looked at her phone to see how Stormy was since she was sleeping in her bedroom.

He looked at her. "You sound like you have regrets."

"Not many. Overall, it's been a great, one-of-a-kind experience working for the world's richest Black family, but it hasn't been a perfect one; but I knew that before I signed up for all of this, like you said." She looked at him. "Is there any truth to what Nika Rose said on her latest video?"

"Fuck that bitch."

She grinned. "You didn't answer my question."

"What's the question?"

She sighed. "Big Teddy, come on now. You know damn well what I'm talking about. We said a while back that we would confide in each other about what goes on in the Royce family since we're both insiders, remember?"

"Yeah, I remember," he replied as he still looked at the ceiling.

"So, I'm listening. I'm in the mood to hear some tea, so spill it."

He shrugged. "I don't know what it is you want me to tell you."

"Tell me about what happened to Chief that night he left Dray's house."

"He left, and Leon and I made sure he left. He was mad and upset, but we made sure he got into his car and got off of this property. He drove off down the driveway as if nothing was wrong. None of us know what happened once he got out of this community."

"So you guys didn't follow him or anything?"

"No. Why would we do that?"

"Just asking because that's what Nika was trying to imply that y'all could've followed him or even hurt him while he was still up there in Dray and Eve's house and one of y'all drove his car and staged it in the ditch to look like an accident."

"Well, that didn't happen. He drove off once he got in his car. Where he went and how he ended up in that ditch, well, we had nothing to do with it. I protect Dray and Eve and their kids and the Royce family, not anyone else. And Leon and all of the other bodyguards do the same. That's our job. That's what we get paid for. And we do our job exceptionally well. You're on the inside with us, Carmella. You need to stop watching that Nika bitch and all of those others out there who talk bad about the Royce family."

"But it's okay for Dray and Eve to watch her all of the time?"

He grinned. "They can watch what they want."

"And so can I. And what I also wanna know is . . . ."

He turned and looked at her. "Wanna know what, Carmella?"

"What I wanna know is will you do anything for Dray like what Nika said?"

He sighed. "Just about."

Juvenile's "Back That Thang Up" featuring Mannie Fresh and Lil Wayne began playing.

"Oh, shit! We ain't done yet!" Carmella said as she got on her hands and knees and started twerking in his face.

He started laughing as he got behind her. "Yeah, I'll fuck your fat ass!"

She laughed even harder. "Fuck it hard, Big Teddy!"

CHAPTER 10

THE EXPOSED

"DRAY!!!" I screamed as I ran down the hall to his office, and it seemed as if it was a mile away each time I walked or ran to it like I was doing.

He ran out of it right before I got to his doors. "What?! What is it, Eve?"

"Turn on one of your TVs!" I said as I was practically out of breath.

He turned on the biggest one that was mounted on the wall between four others. "What's going on, Eve?"

"Search for this video right here," I said, and showed him my phone.

He looked at all of the video selections on the screen. "Don't have to. It's right here. Coincidentally, it came up in my new videos suggestions." He turned it on.

SIA BIJOO'S TEA FOR YOU
BREAKING NEWS!
ELLESSE ROSATI'S BABY CONFIRMED THROUGH
DNA TO BE BASEBALL STAR RIGOR BROWN'S CHILD
—TEAMMATE OF BOYFRIEND CHIEF SMITH

"Told you it was a possibility it wasn't mine," Dray said in a calm voice.

"Do you wanna watch the rest of it?" I asked.

"Sure, why not?"

We continued to watch:

"Hello, everyone, and welcome to my show. For those of you who are new here, I'm Sia Bijoo, social media influencer bringing the social media tea directly to you. Yes, everyone, this has been confirmed on social media just a few hours ago, and I was able to obtain exclusive documentation of it through the DNA lab that conducted the test on Ellesse's baby since her parents wanted proof before they pursued any legal action against Dray Royce for the death of their daughter and her unborn child, their grandchild. As everyone knows, Ellesse was shot and killed by Gina Knight, who was a jail escapee as well as being the ex-girlfriend of Chief Smith, Ellesse's current boyfriend. Gina was eventually killed by the cops as well as Joanna Woodburn, the other jail escapee, which left Brittney Hart to be the only survivor of the three who escaped that day. This all occurred at the yacht docks in front of Royce patriarch Mayson Royce's *Royce II* yacht. Dray and his father Clayton's yachts are docked there as well. This incident occurred almost a month ago. We reached out to Chief Smith to get his reaction to this since Ellesse did say her baby was Dray's, but we have not heard back from him as of yet. We also reached out to Dray and Eve Royce as well but were also met with a non-response."

"Did you get anything from her or her people?" Dray asked me.

"If I did then I totally missed it, but I don't see why I would since everything has to go through Iona before it gets to me so maybe this Sia or her people contacted Iona and she just didn't wanna bother me with it."

Dray checked his phone. "Yeah, that's who everything is supposed to go through. Since I don't have a personal assistant all matters like this go through my lawyers and they didn't contact me about this girl trying to get in touch with me. Who is she?"

"Mill told me she's just some typical social media influencer like she said in the beginning of this video. Nothing special since we would probably know more about her if she had something or done things worth knowing about. I think she's just trying to get herself more out there to be noticed and what better way to do it than to start talking about us?"

"Yeah, you're right about that because I'd never seen her before. Well, I guess we can say we have another video to watch with someone talking about us, huh?"

I sighed. "Yeah, I guess. I'm just glad the baby wasn't yours. I now feel bad confronting her and doing all of that shit was for absolutely nothing. I offered her a $47 million-dollar check and she didn't take it. Either she really thought the baby was yours and knew she could get more money out of you, or she knew it was a possibility it was someone else's and actually had a conscience about not taking the money if it was."

"Well, who knows what she thought. But you didn't know, Eve, and she was at least convincing to you that it was mine. No, I had no right having sex with her where it definitely could've been mine. It doesn't take back what I did."

"Yeah, well, at least you realize that. But Rigor or his wife don't have to deal with the fact that their lives could've been a lot different had Gina not killed Ellesse."

"I wish she would not have killed her because it was flat-out wrong no matter whose baby it was."

"Yeah, you're right. But what would you have done if it was yours, Dray?"

He sighed as he looked down at the floor. He looked up to me giving him a dead-ass-serious stare. He knew I really wanted to know. "Honestly, Eve, I would've tried to reach a settlement with her like what I did for Angela, okay? But you know what happened when it came to that."

"Yeah, I know. I'm just glad this is over, Dray, with in terms of the child not being yours even though Ellesse or the baby didn't survive.

Her parents only wanted to find this out so they could get some money out of someone."

"I know they did, but they're not getting any out of me for a daughter who is not here anymore as well as an unborn grandchild. It's Rigor's problem, not mine."

"For once," I said. I sighed as I shook my head. "What are you gonna do about Chief? You know he's been back at home for weeks now after getting into that accident, but we still don't know what really happened to him when he left this house since he hasn't talked publicly about it. And I know he found out today about Ellesse's baby not being yours after all, but what hurts most is that it still wasn't his as well."

"Well, when he's ready to talk to me then I'll talk. He said I'm not a friend of his and he's not a client of my company anymore, so when I think about it, Eve, there is really nothing for us to talk about."

"I know you don't believe that, Dray. I know you still consider him a friend. I know you won't feel better until you at least try to reach out to him to see how he is and how he feels about what was just exposed today."

"I don't think he wants to talk about that, and I don't blame him. At least now it won't be my ass he wants to beat. Ellesse was exposed for having multiple affairs with other men behind Chief's back, but Chief told me he cheated on her a lot, too."

I shook my head. "Well, she'll never be able to do it again. I hope other women learn from what'd happened to her and her unborn child."

"Yeah, I hope so, too."

CHAPTER 11

THE CLIENT

"I don't know why I'm so nervous standing here, but I am," I said, as Dray and I stood at the front door of Chief's house waiting for someone to answer. He accepted Dray's wanting to talk to him about what'd happened and wanted me to come along with him, and I had to admit I was very surprised. But I was more nervous over the fact at what'd happened the last time I was here, and it was something that would always be etched in my mind.

"I told you, Eve, I still consider him my friend," he said, as I could see that he seemed a little nervous as well. I looked back at Auer and Leon as they sat in Dray's car. Dray required them to come with us.

I could feel him staring at me, and my eyes met his. "What?"

"Are you okay?"

"Yeah. Why do you ask?"

"Because of the last time you were over here . . . alone."

I sighed. "I don't wanna talk about it. It's been done for years now."

"I'm sorry I made you do it."

I looked at him. "Why are you sorry now, Dray? Because you lost Chief as a business and personal client? Would you be sorry if he was still with your company?"

Before he could answer me, a petite woman in a grey and white traditional maid's uniform answered the door. "Hello, Mr. and Mrs. Royce."

"Hello, Mayra," Dray and I said.

She led us to the recreation room where Chief sat watching TV. "Go on in," she said with a smile.

"Chief!" Dray said in a pitiful attempt to sound upbeat as if nothing at all had happened.

I instantly caught secondhand embarrassment.

Chief turned around from watching TV. "Hey, Dray, Eve. What's up?" He got up wearing Versace Baroque gold and black silk pajamas. He was clearly unshaven and looked overall disheveled, and it seemed as if he didn't care about how he looked to anyone at the moment, and in a lot of ways, I really couldn't blame him.

"Glad you wanted to talk after what'd happened at my house the last time we saw each other," Dray said.

"Yeah, well, as you can see that I'm fine and still alive. Damn animal ran in front of me while I was driving home that made me run off the fuckin' road that night. That's what really happened. Have a seat," he said to us, as he stared at me.

Normally, we would've hugged him or whatever kind gesture we would all exchange with each other, but I could still feel the tension with him that he had with Dray, therefore, he seemed as if he had it with me. I felt this was guilt by association at its finest. I just didn't think he was changing his mind about anything. I even had to wonder what we were doing over here to begin with because it seemed as if he didn't wanna talk to us after all.

"Y'all want a drink?" he asked.

"No thanks," I answered for me and Dray.

Dray grinned at me. "Just some water, man."

"It's over in the bar refrigerator. You know where it's at," Chief replied as he glared at him.

Dray gave a surprised look that he couldn't hide, and got up and went over to the bar refrigerator to get a bottle of water. He knew Chief was still upset.

Chief stared me down as he slowly took a sip of his drink.

"I'm sorry I lost you as a client, but especially as a friend," Dray said, and took a fast, nervous sip of his water.

"Shit happens," Chief replied, and took another sip of his drink. "Too much shit has happened, especially to me."

"What's gonna happen to Rigor, man?" Dray asked.

"He was traded; I don't know where and I don't care. I have the power on that team, not him or anyone else. My agent told me that his agent didn't hesitate to try and find him another team because he knew I no longer wanted to work with him even though Ellesse and their unborn baby are dead. Doesn't matter. It's the principle of everything that has happened. I hope he gets traded to the worst team ever right now," Chief said, and took another sip of his drink. "And I thought all of this bad shit was behind me. I honestly didn't know if she was gonna be found alive or not. I actually thought she was already dead, so I was surprised to see her run off of your grandfather's yacht that day, Dray."

"I'm sorry that my bodyguards put her down in there, man. I really am. I had nothing to do with it and knew nothing about it until they told me," Dray said, and this was the second time he'd told him he hadn't.

"Who's they?" Chief asked as he kept his glare on him.

Dray looked at me; I stared passively at the TV.

"The bodyguards that I eventually fired, man. And they were fired immediately when they confessed to me what they did."

"You still haven't told me why they did what they did since you claim you had nothing to do with it," he reminded him.

I looked at Dray.

"They told me they were there at my yacht at the time and found her wandering around there on the docks. They asked her what was she doing there and she told them she was looking for me because she needed to talk to me about something important. They told me that Auer and Leon told them that she was pregnant by me, so they thought they were helping me by putting her in my grandfather's yacht. I don't know what their point was of doing that," Dray said.

I knew he'd made up everything to Chief as he went along.

Chief shook his head and took another sip of his drink. "Something still doesn't make sense. But Ellesse obviously told you she was pregnant—thinking that it was yours, obviously, since you're the richest Black man in the world—and you must've told Auer and Leon or they overheard it or something."

"Yeah, something like that. Look, man, I know I'm the cause of everything that has happened, but I still don't wanna think that I can't make things right between us."

"Yeah? How are you gonna do that?" Chief asked.

I looked at Dray because I knew he really wanted Chief back as a client, but most of all as a friend.

"I honestly don't know, man. You tell me."

Chief sighed. "You know, I told your assistants to put a hold on my accounts being transferred to Gilcrest."

"What?!" Dray said, as he tried not to get excited.

"Seriously, Chief?" I asked.

"Yeah, seriously, Eve," he replied, and then once again stared me down as he took another sip of his drink.

"They didn't tell me," Dray said.

"That's because I told them not to tell you. I told them to put a hold on it when I found out that Rigor was the father of Ellesse's child, and not you, but especially not me. But it still doesn't make everything right."

"I know it doesn't," Dray said. "What can I do to make things right?"

"I'm happy you asked that," Chief replied. "It's been fucked up for me. Real fucked up. And I'm tired of shit being fucked up for me."

"That's why we're here, Chief. We want you to feel better," I said.

"Exactly," Dray said. "I mean it from the bottom of my heart, man. You know I love you and still consider you my friend, man."

I'd never heard Dray talk like this before. I knew he really, truly felt bad about what he'd done, and Chief had never done anything to him that made him do what he did to him. But I knew Dray wanted him back as a client bad since he was one of his company's biggest.

Chief glared at him, and then turned his attention to me. "Remember what I wrote in my book to you, Eve, at my book signing?"

To Eve,

Glad to see you're fine.
Let's do it again sometime.

All my Best,
Chief

Dray looked at me since he knew about Chief's book—and we were in bed when I actually read a good portion of it—but I never showed him the inscription and for obvious reasons.

"No," I lied, because I remembered it word-for-word.

Chief grinned; he could see right through me. "I'd love to still be a client, Dray. Y'all have done the best for me. It was you, your dad, and all the others at Royce Investments that made me the richest man in sports. No one compares to you all."

"Great!" Dray said in an excited tone.

"Wonderful!" I said with true excitement, and I could tell I was even more excited than Dray who was trying to remain calm.

"So there's something I want done for me," Chief said.

"Anything, man," Dray said.

Chief grinned. "I hope you mean that, man."

"I do," Dray replied with a smile.

But not for one second was I smiling. I locked eyes with Chief; a sickening feeling came all over me.

"No, man, you don't understand what I'm saying. I hope you mean it. *I really hope* you mean it."

Dray looked at him, then looked at him again. I knew he knew exactly what Chief was saying. He could read all between the lines and so could I.

"Dray . . ." My voice trailed off. He looked at me as he raised his eyebrows at me in a non-verbal way to continue with what I was saying. "Remember what you said to me? *Remember?*" I stressed as I started to breathe heavy.

"This is the only time I'm gonna allow this in our marriage. You have to do it. I already told him that you would."

"No, Eve. I don't know what you're talking about."

"The hell you don't, Dray. You know *exactly* what I'm talking about. *You know* what you said, Dray. Don't sit there and act as if you don't have any idea what I'm talking about."

"What are you talking about, Eve?" Chief asked as he stared at me, and then took another sip of his drink.

"Dray knows," I replied as I tried hard not to let tears well up in my eyes. "DRAY!!"

Dray looked at me, and then lowered his head.

Chief looked at Dray, then at me.

I shook my head as I was now about to explode in anger. "I didn't cause this shit this time, Dray, *YOU* DID! This is *your* fuckup! *Not mine*! I had *nothing* to do with it this time! Don't . . . don't do this to me, Dray . . . *DON'T! You said* I didn't have to do this again!"

He looked at me. "Do it."

"DRAY!!!"

Chief slowly took off his pajama top and was now completely topless. He walked over to me as Dray still sat in his seat, and gently pulled me up off the couch. "It won't take that long this time."

"DRAY!!!" I yelled again.

Chief began to give me soft, sexy kisses all over my neck as Dray got off the couch and turned and walked towards the door and out of the room. "You smell so good. I've been waiting for the perfect time for us to do this again."

I remained quiet as I couldn't believe this was happening between us again, and this time I was not the cause of it at all.

"Do you like me, Eve?" he asked, as he continued to kiss me all over my face and neck.

"Yes, I like you, Chief. And just because I like you, we shouldn't have to do this again."

"Why not? Your husband still has me as a client now. You should be just as happy as him."

"I am."

He lifted up my chin. "Show me."

We slowly leaned into each other and began kissing as if we were deeply in love as our tongues sloshed around in each other's mouths like some horny teens who talked or texted on their phones about wanting to have sex with each other and were finally doing it.

And I couldn't believe I was doing this with Chief.

Again.

But for some reason, I was so attracted to him at this moment, but I felt I only was because he was remaining a business and personal client at my husband's company, and I had to show my full gratitude.

My pussy had never gotten as hot and as wet this fast, and I was trying not to let the guilt of it plague me as I tried to push it out of my subconscious about the fact that I was attracted to Chief more than I wanted to admit that I was. I felt I was doing this more for pleasure than for business this second time, even though the latter was most definitely true and always would be.

He pulled down my sweatpants and dove his hand directly into my panties and rubbed my clit as he continued to smother me with those soft and sexy kisses. "Damn, you feel good, baby. So soft, hot, wet, and so fast. You really do like me, huh?"

"Yes," I replied as we started kissing once again as I was now only in my tee as I jumped on him and he fell on the couch with me on top of him, and he immediately went inside of me. "Fuck my hot and wet cunt, baby."

"Don't stop talking dirty to me, baby," he said as he breathed heavy while he hammered me hard as I laid my head on his neck as his soft unshaven beard and scent of his cologne made my nipples so hard they almost burst right through my bra. He reached up inside the back of my tee and unhooked my strapless bra for me, and I threw it on the ground. He pulled up the front of my tee and pulled it off of me, and began giving me some of the best tongue-to-tit sex I'd ever had. "You like this, baby?"

"Fuck yeah! I fuckin' love it!" I said as I breathed in a heavy breath as I felt myself ready to cum and that rarely happened from this type of sex. I started to moan louder as I breathed heavy and let out a loud scream as I dropped my head back on to his shoulder.

"You came, didn't you?" he said as he smiled at me.

"Yeah, I did. And that rarely happens when a man sucks on my tits," I said as I still breathed heavy.

"I'm the best at it," he said with a smile.

We began kissing again, and this was the most I'd ever kissed another man besides Dray. Something was taking over me right now in a way that it hadn't when we had done this the first time here. It was amazing how I could go from not wanting to do this at all with him to having hot, butt-naked sex with him once again, and I was enjoying it more this time than the first time. I guess we both needed someone to make us feel good with everything we'd been through, and we didn't go through everything what we'd gone through together, but everything always seemed connected.

I laid on my back as I pulled him up towards me and on top of me as he went inside of me fast and hard. "Fuck me hard, baby! Fuck yeah!" I said as my moaning echoed as he went as fast as he could and let out the loudest moan as he pulled out of me fast and came all over the floor. He quickly wiped himself off and put his dick in my mouth.

"Suck that shit, baby," he said as he breathed heavy as I moved my head in a fast motion in all different directions. "You're fuckin' good, baby, FUCK!" he said, and quickly took his dick out of my mouth and came once again. "Let me tongue-fuck your pussy, baby."

I thrusted my hips up and down as I held my hands on the back of his head as he sucked on my hot and soft clit so fast and tongue-fucked so deep into me so good that I was convinced this was a beautiful, natural gift of his because not every man could do it right. My screams almost blew out the windows as I came.

"Your pussy tastes like candy, baby. Just as sweet and beautiful as you."

"Thank you, Chief," I said with a smile as held me as if he was Dray.

"I hate to cut this short, but I know Dray is waiting for you."

"I actually wanted this to last longer," I admitted.

He smiled. "Are you serious, Eve?"

"Yeah, I am. I wouldn't say anything I don't mean."

"Damn, you're beautiful, Eve. I wish I had a wife like you." He leaned into me and we began kissing again. He softly rubbed my pussy as he stared at me.

I began moaning and started breathing heavy once again as I opened my legs wider. I closed my eyes as I couldn't believe I'd let this happen once again. I opened them . . . .

To Dray staring back at me with his arms crossed!

I looked at Chief as he immediately stopped and slowly got up and put his pajama pants back on. I didn't say a word as I quickly got dressed, as I reminded myself that I didn't get caught cheating on him. He wanted me to do this again to keep Chief as a client for good, but the look on his face told me a whole different story. It was one thing for him to make me do this again, but it was a whole other thing for him to see us butt naked in each other's arms as Chief was still sexually satisfying me and I was actually enjoying it.

He looked jealous and full of regret that he allowed this to happen again.

I sighed as I walked towards him as Chief stayed where he was as he waited for us to say something to each other first.

"I love you," Dray said.

That was the last thing I expected for him to say. "I love you, too."

"Go on out to the car. I'll be out in a few minutes."

I turned and looked at Chief as he stared right at me. "Bye."

He nodded with a smile. "Bye, Eve. Thank you."

I walked out of the room, but quickly stood around the corner to hear what they were about to say.

"Thanks for letting me do it again with her, man."

"I was wondering why it was taking longer than I thought it would. It's obvious that she had no problems doing it again."

"She told me she didn't."

"Glad to have kept you as a client, man."

"I'm glad to still be one. Thank your wife as well."

"Of course."

"I wanna get her a gift for what went down tonight between us again, if you don't mind?"

"No, I don't mind."

"What does she like?"

"She likes flowers."

Minutes later, I walked over to the car where Leon stood with the door open for me; curiosity was all over his face.

"Thank you," I said, and got inside.

Minutes later, Dray got in on his side as Auer shut the door. He looked at me. "Are you okay?"

I looked in the rearview mirror and saw Leon staring back at me. "I'm fine."

"I thought so. You seemed very comfortable."

Auer and Leon looked at each other as I could tell they tried hard not to look back at me.

"Not here, Dray," I said, as I stared out the window.

"So, is Chief still a client of yours, Dray?" Leon asked.

Dray looked at me. "He most definitely still is."

CHAPTER 12

THE BLAMING

I stepped out of the shower to Dray sitting on one of my bathroom benches staring at me.

"Chief's right. You are beautiful, Eve."

I nodded with a smile as I still toweled myself off. I put on my panties then pajamas as he watched me. He followed me back to our bedroom. I sighed. "What is it, Dray?"

"Are you attracted to him, Eve?"

I sighed again as I got in bed. "Why are you asking me this, Dray? I did what you wanted me to do for the second time even though this time I was not the cause of anything."

"That's where you're wrong."

I looked at him. "I don't wanna start a fight, okay? I'm tired. I was not expecting to have sex with Chief tonight for the second time when we went over there."

"Well, I had to do what I had to do for our livelihood."

"No, *I* did what we supposedly had to do for our livelihood, Dray, not you, even though our livelihood is in the billions and billions. If it was so important to keep him then *you* should've had sex with him. We would've still done just fine without him as a client."

"I'm not gay, Eve, you know that all-too well. And neither is Chief. And don't always be so sure of that about us being fine without him as a client. Every client is important to me and my company—business and individual. Every single one. You're more than likely right about us being fine without him, but nothing is a sure thing. I think he would've lost money had he went through with the transfer to Gilcrest, and I was gonna do whatever I could to make sure that didn't happen, for us and for him."

"Well, I'm the cause of him staying with your company, Dray. At least you can thank me for it."

"I would thank you."

"*Would?* And why do you say it like that?"

"Because I feel this second time that you did it more for pleasure than for business."

"Bullshit. I'm going to sleep," I said, and turned over.

"Not until we're done talking."

"I don't wanna talk about this anymore. What's done is done, right?"

"Nothing is ever fully done."

"I don't feel like going around in an argumentative circle with you, Dray. It's clear you were watching us for those last few minutes and you felt some kind of way about it. How long were you standing there?"

"For a few minutes," he said, as he glared at me.

"You never left the house the whole time?"

"Never."

"Where were you?"

"Around," he said, as he passively looked at the TV.

"Goodnight," I said.

"*I said* I'm not done talking, Eve. You're trying to avoid accepting responsibility for why you had to do this again because you are just as much to blame for it as I am, and you don't even realize it."

I turned over and looked at him. "Okay, Dray. Tell me what I don't realize. Why did I have to do this again with Chief? How am I to blame for having to do this again with him, huh? I'm listening."

"How did Ellesse end up at my yacht, huh?"

I sighed. "You were still the cause of it, Dray. If you didn't have sex with her then she would not have texted you to tell you she was pregnant. It was clear she thought the baby was yours."

"Yeah, it was clear she did, but in the end it wasn't. And she only ended up at my yacht because *you* answered the text she'd sent me about her being pregnant and saying I was the father, so *you* told her to meet me at my yacht, and she did it thinking you were me. You're the one who put everything in motion, Eve, for everything to have happened and went down the way it ultimately did. You had more of a significant role in it than you think you did—than you want to admit you did—and you know it. Even though we found out that Rigor was in fact the father, everything that happened at my gramps's yacht that day started because, like I said, *you* told her to meet you there pretending you were me. Of course no one knew Gina and the other two were gonna escape from jail and end up at the yacht docks, but they did, and shit happened like it always does. And why they chose to run there? Well, only Brittney can tell us now, and she hasn't said shit. But no one would've ever been there had you not told Ellesse to meet you there pretending to be me."

I looked at him. "It's all over, isn't it? I let myself get fucked and sucked on by your biggest and best client once again just to keep him from going through with the transfer to Gilcrest. So it's over, right?"

He sighed. "Let's hope so."

"I don't wanna hear that shit."

"Then don't start any. All of this could've been prevented, Eve, and you know it."

"And I can tell you not to start any either."

He let out a sarcastic chuckle, and then turned a daunting gaze my way which left me completely unfazed. "Do you have feelings for him, Eve? Like the way you have for me? Or like the way you have for Leon?"

"Stop, Dray."

"You didn't answer my question."

"Yes, I did. I told you to stop."

"Is that a yes?"

"It means stop with the ridiculous questions you already know the answers to."

He grinned. "I just wanna hear you say it, that's all."

"You're just trying to start shit, that's all."

"I'm not starting anything, Eve. All I wanna do is confirm what I saw."

"And what exactly did you see, Dray, that you haven't seen? You always find a way to catch me with someone else since I'm always out there sleeping with every man out there."

"I never said that, Eve."

"Well, you make me feel that way, Dray, and I'm tired of it. You know, we can keep blaming each other over who caused what and why I had to do what I had to do to keep one of your company's biggest clients, but nothing is gonna stop being so fucked up for us if we don't stop doing things we know we shouldn't be doing."

"I agree."

We stared in a passive silence at the TV for a few minutes.

"You were very comfortable."

"And you didn't have to say that shit in front of Leon and Auer. They knew what you meant by it."

"They know not to say anything."

"That's not the point, Dray. They obviously know I had sex with Chief again and I didn't have to tell them."

"You're not supposed to. What goes on between us is our business."

I sighed. "Yeah, everything for business."

"It's why you have billions in your bank accounts, remember that."

I sighed as I shook my head. "Anything else you want me to remember?"

"That'll be the last time you and Chief will have that kind of involvement with each other."

"You said that the last time."

"I mean it this time," he said as he stared me down. "He's staying with us for good, so get out any kind of sexual desires that's still making your pussy wet about him right now."

"Goodnight, Dray," I said, as I turned over.

"I just got one more thing to say," he said, as he stared mundanely at the TV.

"Make it quick."

"There's a reason why I'm saying all of this, Eve."

"And what's the reason, Dray?"

"I think Chief is in love with you."

CHAPTER 13

THE LOVE

I JUMPED UP OUT OF A DEEP SLEEP WHILE STILL IN BED TO THE beginning of Dru Hill's "How Deep Is Your Love" blasting throughout the room. I looked at Dray as he put on his tie while he stared back at me. "Very funny."

"Nothing funny about it, Eve. In fact, I'm having a meeting with Chief this morning."

"About what?"

"About my appreciation of him staying a client of ours. My dad will be attending the meeting as well."

"I hope I don't come up in it, Dray."

He grinned. "It's all business, isn't it?"

"Dray! I'm serious!"

"So am I." He came over to me and kissed me on my head. "Have a great day, baby."

Minutes later, I stood in Layton's bedroom as he still slept as I looked out the window while Dray walked to the car with his sunglasses on while Auer held open the door for him. I loved looking at how gorgeous and sexy he looked every morning while he walked to his car, but I couldn't see him as being that way this morning. He knew just how to get under my skin and so early in the morning at that.

I looked over at Layton as he was now awake smiling at me. "Good morning!" I said in my sweet voice to him as I picked him up and gave him kisses all over his face as he laughed. Sometimes I felt he was the only one besides Mill who kept me sane.

"Eve? These just came for you," Leon said, as he brought in a huge bouquet of fuchsia pink roses in a gigantic black box.

"Wow, those are beautiful," I replied as I looked inside of them for a card.

Thanks again for another unforgettable time.

Chief

I looked up to Leon staring back at me.

"Who are they from?" he asked with a smile.

"Chief," I replied, and put the card to the side.

He nodded. "So, it's clear he was happy to see you again at his house because he also sent you this." He handed me a box. "They were all standing at the door when I got here, Eve. The person who had this box had an armed guard standing with them. They said they knew you and knew who I was, so they let me sign it for you."

"Thank you, Leon," I replied with a smile. "Um, can you take these flowers up to my office?"

"Sure, Eve."

I looked to see if he was out of sight and opened the box . . . .

"She likes flowers."

To a stunning Van Cleef & Arpels Flowerlace necklace in 18 karat white gold and diamonds. This was from the high jewelry collection, and I knew this because I had a few pieces from this particular collection, but I didn't have this necklace which was a whopping $201,000. I knew this was a gift from Chief, the kind of gifts I got from Dray during special times of the year or when he was being naughty and thought he could make it up to me with some high jewelry. I'd never received any type of high jewelry from any other man besides Dray *and the other one,* but I wanted to keep him suppressed out of my subconscious.

I never expected to get something this nice from someone I just had a second sexual business transaction with, as I called it. He was serious. And now I had to believe that there was definitely some truth to what Dray told me before we finally got to sleep last night. Since I was wearing a solid V-neck tee, I decided to try it on. I put it on and went to the mirror in the foyer. "This is stunning."

"It is," Leon said with a smile.

It seemed as if he came out of nowhere.

"That was fast," I said, as I still stood with the necklace around my neck.

"I take it that's from Chief, too? Must have been a hell of a night last night."

I gave him an offensive look. "I don't wanna talk about it." I walked away and back into the kitchen.

"Eve, I'm sorry. You know I didn't mean to offend you."

"*I said* I don't wanna talk about it."

"Okay," he replied as he gave me a look of concern. He looked at his watch. "Um, we should get going since you're meeting Mill for lunch at Grayson's."

"I know," I said, and put the necklace back in its box.

"Are you okay?"

"Yeah, I'm fine. Let's go."

"Wow, Eve. This necklace is something else! This is definitely something Dray would've bought you," Mill said, as she stared at my gift from Chief as it still sat in its box. "I think Dray's right."

"Right about what?"

"I think Chief is in love with you."

I sighed. "Don't you start it, too."

"Well, even though he can afford to give a woman these kinds of gifts just as much as Dray can, I just don't think he does. When a man gives a woman a gift like this, Eve, he's either hiding something and feels guilty about it, or he's in love. I think it's the latter."

"I just don't wanna think about that being a possibility. Like I told you, I honestly didn't think I was gonna have to do it again with him, and then Dray told me to 'Do it' right in front of him. I thought he was kidding at first. Then it was weird because when Dray supposedly 'left' I started to become really attracted to Chief and started going off sexually on him and I didn't think I would do what I was gonna do. Then when we were in bed last night, Dray and I started blaming each other for why I had to do what I did again. I just want all of this to stop, Mill."

"I know you do, Eve. But are you attracted to Chief?"

"Dray asked me the same thing." I sighed and took a sip of my coffee.

She stared at me in suspense. "Well?"

"Well, I don't know how I feel. I'm just so confused about everything right now. I just want all of this drama to stop."

"I think it's stopped for now. I mean, no one has to worry about Gina ever again, and it's unfortunate what happened to Ellesse, but it happened and there's nothing anyone can do about it. Chief is now moving on with his life as hard as that is, but he knows he has to. And it's clear to me and to Dray that you could quite possibly be his new love interest."

"Please don't say that, Mill."

"Well, you know I'm only gonna tell you the truth in what I'm thinking. Him getting you a necklace like that is very telling. I mean, I'm sure he didn't get his wives any high jewelry like that."

"I don't know that, maybe he did."

"Well, maybe, maybe not, but I guarantee you he probably didn't get any woman he wasn't married to anything like that, especially a woman who's married to someone else."

"That part you're probably right about, Mill."

"Eve, you're on a whole other level than 99.9% of women out there. And you're a Black woman at that. You're just looked at differently from the rest of us."

"I still believe I'm just plain-old Eve."

"You're anything but that and you know it. Because you're Dray Royce's wife, you're attracting more wealthy men to you."

"But what's funny, Mill, is that before Dray? I seemed to have never been able to attract the type of men then that I do now. It's just so unexplainable. Dray gave me a chance with him and he changed my life forever because of it, but that would've never happened had I not taken the chance and wrote to him. But since I did, it's like now all of these wealthy men—regardless of race, but especially Black ones—are now noticing me. Being with Dray really has put me in a spotlight and in circles like no other, I know that's for sure."

"And it's the best spotlight and circles a woman can be in. It's not perfect—I know, because I've been with you for this whole journey—but it's better than struggling and living a life you never wanted to live. Every woman should strive for a life like yours, Eve, but some ruin themselves before they even give themselves a chance. Not every woman qualifies like you did to live the life you live. Hate to be harsh, but it is what it is."

"Very true. But it's unfortunate that there's still not enough Drays or Claytons or Maysons or Jeffs to go around for the ones who do qualify. Hell, there's not many men of other races on their level of wealth. They're truly one of a kind when it comes to their wealth and them all being Black makes it even more so. I will never take living like this for granted or the love I have for Dray and his love for me—but I am human, I make mistakes. I have feelings I know I shouldn't have."

"And that's all a part of being human, Eve." She looked at her phone. "Oh my god!"

"What?"

"Um . . . I think Chief is very, very happy he stayed with your husband's company, Eve."

"Why is that?"

"He's the newest Black billionaire."

CHAPTER 14

THE MEMBER

<u>SIA BIJOO'S TEA FOR YOU</u>
BREAKING NEWS!
THERE'S A NEW BLACK BILLIONAIRE IN THE BLACK
COMMUNITY!
BASEBALL STAR CHIEF SMITH JOINS THE EXCLU-
SIVE BLACK BILLIONAIRE MEN'S CLUB
SAYS "IT'S A DREAM ACHIEVED"

"Hello, everyone, and welcome to my show, I'm Sia Bijoo, bringing all of the social media tea to you. But this is not gossip, this is very real and very much needs to be talked about because I think it's too important not to be. Having another Black billionaire in the Black community is very powerful and shows the positive direction Black men are in when faced with numerous challenges and tragedies such as what baseball star Chief Smith has faced. Everyone knows about the latest with the two women he was involved with, but what most probably didn't know was that Chief probably would not have become a billionaire had he not stayed at Royce Investments. Yes, you heard that only from me, and that is not fake tea, that is the actual truth. Chief was all set to leave Royce Investments because what'd happened between his girlfriend at the time, Ellesse Rosati, who as everyone knows was pregnant and killed by his ex-girlfriend and jail escapee Gina Knight. Dray convinced Chief to stay with his company, and look what happens? He becomes a billionaire because, according to what I was told by an associate who deals with Royce business matters, a stock he invested in shot up over 20,000%, sending Chief into billionaire status.

"Look, ladies, I don't mean to get off subject here, but Chief is single. He's been married twice before and does have children, but if you want a chance at the newest Black billionaire who just joined the elite ranks of Dray Royce, Clayton Royce, Mayson Royce, and Jeff Vick, just to name the very few, then here's your chance! But I also have to warn you all. There's a rumor that he does have a love interest, but no one is saying who it might be. Wow, that was pretty fast!"

DRAY LOOKED AT ME. "WHO IS THIS CHICK? AND HOW IS SHE finding out stuff that most people don't know?"

"I have no idea, Dray. But it's clear she's finding out because like you said, most people don't know the kind of stuff she is saying. There's just something different about her than that Nika bitch and all of the others who talk about us; I just don't know what it is."

"Yeah, that's what I think, too. But I also think that love interest Chief has is in you."

"Dray. Come on now."

"Come on what, Eve? Huh? What man buys a woman a $201,000 necklace that's not his wife? Hell, I've only bought *you* high jewelry. I never bought any of my girlfriends in the past stuff like that because I didn't want them to get the wrong idea that I was about to propose to them."

"Well, that's why you still have the money you have. You could've lost millions on spending it on girlfriends who you never had any intentions on marrying."

"Yeah, you're right. I was only gonna spend millions and millions on my wife, which has now turned into billions."

"And I take nothing for granted."

"That's why I married you and not any of them."

We kissed.

"But I want that to be the last thing he buys you, Eve."

I sighed. "Dray. I'm not expecting any more gifts from Chief."

"I hope not," he said, as he stared at the TV. "I just put him into Black billionaire status. He can officially have any woman he wants, now and forever."

"And just to think he was gonna leave your company."

"He went on instinct and stopped the transfer before it happened. Had he not done that, he wouldn't be a billionaire today. His timing was absolutely crucial, and he acted on it."

"So he's gonna be the keynote speaker at the Black Billionaire Men's Invitational Business Summit?"

"Absolutely, since it's usually either the richest Black man in the world or the newest Black billionaire that gives the speech. I'm glad I don't have to give it this year since I had to for the last few years," he said with a sexy smile.

"And you're not fooling me, Dray, you love doing it."

"Who wouldn't? It's truly an honor."

I smiled. "Yes, it is. I just look forward to the party later on that night since the summit is for you men, you Black billionaire men or ones who are close to being like you all."

"And it's always one of the best."

CHAPTER 15

THE USED-TO-BE'S

"Look, I'm tired of you laying around here feeling sorry for yourself. You need to get yourself together and get another job. You have a child to support," Lupe said, Jose's girlfriend.

"Don't bother me," he said, and turned back over on the couch.

"Look, I'm not gonna stand for this. You know damn well you can get another job, Jose."

"That was the best job I ever had, Lupe! *Ever*! What part of that don't you understand? Damn! Leave me alone!"

She sighed. "I'm not leaving you alone. You've been in a shitty mood since Dray fired you and Brock, and I'm tired of it. We can't live like this, Jose, and you know it. As soon as you told me you were fired, I went out and got a job—but I can't support us both and our daughter on what I make. You need to be a man and get the hell up from that couch and get back out there and work. Being like this for this long is only making things worse for you. It's not gonna get any better if you don't put back in the effort to do what you know you gotta do, and you know it."

He turned and looked at her. "You tell me what kind of job I can get after being fired by Dray? Everyone knows the story and everyone knows who they are. The Royces have connections everywhere so no one is gonna hire me anywhere no matter what kind of job it is. Like I said, that was the best job I ever had. I'm done."

"You're anything but done. I don't wanna hear that shit. I'm not in the mood for it. I'm not gonna stand here and let you feel sorry for yourself for the rest of your life. What's done is done about what happened. It's time to move on. It's clear Dray is not gonna rehire you or Brock. The two of you made a costly mistake. The Royces don't play; you both knew that even before you both did what you did. Is the new Black billionaire Chief Smith hiring?"

"Are you serious, Lupe? There's no way Chief is gonna hire us to protect him. Him and Dray are practically best friends. Too much of a conflict of interest. Brock and I put his pregnant girlfriend down in Dray's grandfather's yacht; how's that gonna work out? Huh? I don't know what the hell I'm gonna do, okay? I don't wanna talk anymore."

A half hour later, Jose still laid on the couch as Lupe approached him.

"Someone's here to see you."

"I don't wanna see anyone."

"Too bad because you're going to. I've already had enough of this bullshit."

He sighed. "Who is it?"

Brock walked into the room with a pack of Jose's favorite beer. "Thirsty?"

Jose barely formed a smile. "In more ways than one."

Lupe smiled broadly. "I'll order some pizzas."

Fifteen minutes later, Jose and Brock indulged in their favorite comfort food.

"You know, right now we would be in a meeting for the Black Billionaire Men's Invitational Business Summit and the party the next day that's in a few days," Brock said, and took a bite of his pizza.

"I know, man. I still have it on my phone as being on schedule. I guess it's just a lot of wishful thinking on my part that we're gonna somehow get rehired. I was thinking since they made an exception in Leon's case then they would make an exception in ours."

"Yeah, and that's *really* wishful thinking, man, considering the fact that Leon found a missing woman and child who happened to be the wife and child of Dray; we hid a woman who was then reported missing. She would've never been reported missing if we didn't do what we did. We're done, man."

Jose shook his head. "I still feel like I'm in a nightmare. Stupidest thing I ever done."

"Me too. If I knew it was gonna cause all of that then I would've just let her go and she would probably still be alive."

"Yeah, we should've just let her go. But should've, could've, would've ain't gonna get us anywhere now."

"Unfortunately," Brock said. "And because of that reason, I just sold my Dodge Charger last week. Damn, I loved that car. Brand new when I bought it and everything and less than two years old. Was only able to get it because I was a Royce bodyguard. We only lived in that amazing 8,000 square-foot home owned by Dray because we were his top bodyguards along with Auer and Leon. What better job could a bodyguard have, you know? I see the reality now that I'm back in that tiny-ass apartment with Emily. No one is gonna pay me what Dray paid us, man."

"I knew that when I first got the job that's why I was hoping I wouldn't lose it. I honestly never thought Dray was gonna fire us over what we did. I thought we were gonna at least get suspended."

"Me too. But that girl ended up in there because of us then she ended up dead by someone else. It's just too much stigma attached to us for what we did, man. And I heard he told Chief it was us who put her in there."

"Well, if he told him, he's not lying because we did. Dray was not the cause of us putting her in his grandfather's yacht since he didn't tell us to do it. We just did that shit on our own. We thought at the time that it was the right thing to do. We didn't know what he wanted us to do with her and we didn't ask him," Jose said, and took a sip of his beer.

"But she was still alive, man! We wouldn't have kept her down in there forever. Damn!"

"Have you called Saadiq?"

Brock nodded. "About a million times, man. He finally blocked me, and had a certified letter sent to my apartment from the Royces' lawyers telling me to leave him alone. I guess he's repped by them, too, even though he's the Royce Security Operations Executive Manager." He got out his phone and showed a picture of the certified letter sent to him.

"Damn, he was serious," Jose said. "It's just hard for me to move on, man. Lupe's been constantly on my ass since being fired. I got a two-year-old daughter to support and pretty much blew all the money I made working for Dray on stupid shit. I have nothing to show for."

"Speaking about a child to support, I sold my car for a reason."

Jose turned and looked at him. "No way, man."

"Yeah, you talk about bad timing? Emily is a few weeks pregnant; she just found out. There's a lot of shit I need to figure out, man, and I'll do anything to get my job back because no one is gonna pay us that kind of money. I'm gonna try and talk to Saadiq again, but if he rejects my wanting to speak to him then I just don't wanna be responsible for my actions."

"It's not that serious, man, but I'm in a desperate situation, too. Right now, I just don't care about much but getting my job back, so if it doesn't happen then I don't know what I'm capable of."

Lupe walked into the room. "I'm surprised there's still enough for me."

"Have at it, baby," Jose said, and took another slice.

She sat down next to him and grabbed a slice.

"I got something to show you, Lupe. I already showed Jose."

CHAPTER 16

THE SUMMIT

"Words cannot express the way I feel right now as I stand before all of you elite gentlemen who are the one percent of the one percent. To stand up here and know that it was not an easy climb makes it all worthwhile, and hard work most definitely pays off. The old saying always rings true about that fact that anything worth doing is worth doing well, and that it takes time to see and achieve your dreams, and being the newest Black billionaire in the Black community is something I never even fathomed when I first started my career as a pro-baseball player at the age of 20; I just never knew if I was gonna have a career-ending injury and didn't know if I was gonna be good at any business ventures if the unfortunate happened. Luckily, I was blessed to never have the unfortunate happen and be good at being a player and at business ventures as well as investing what I earned with Royce Investments since I began my career, and that is the reason why I'm standing up here giving this keynote speech."

Dray, Clayton, and Mayson nodded with a smile as they sat at a table up on stage in the Mayson Royce Conference Room along with Jeff Vick, and this table was reserved for the Black billionaire men only. Many of the low-to-high nine-figure men gazed up on the stage and saw what was possible, and knew that any one of them could be sitting up there next to the Royce men along with Jeff Vick, and now Chief Smith.

Chief continued. "With all of the tragedies that I've endured recently as well as in the past, I always kept my eye on the prize, and that was creating more wealth beyond my wildest dreams. I wanted my kids to see what was possible in life beyond sports, and wanted to be that example for them, and not have them look to someone else for that example. When my sons ask me can they become anything they want as a Black man, they know they can look at me for that answer. Any one of you gentlemen sitting down there right now can be up here on this stage giving this keynote speech. You've made it this far, and just being invited to this summit is something very special. We didn't have the head start that a lot of other people did on our path to great wealth and prosperity, but we made it, and we can go as far as we can and want with it. Nothing has stopped us before, so nothing will ever stop us now as nothing will ever stop our families and our future generations as we continue to produce generational wealth as well as teach generational wealth so it can keep being passed on. We're showing them how it's done. Always. Thank you all."

This year's Summit attendees—which included Harrison Moore, a 19-year-old nine-figure-earning young man dubbed the Socks King for creating basic and trendy socks that didn't snag holes in them—gave Chief a standing ovation as well as the Royce men. He nodded with a smile as photographers took pictures of him as he stood at the podium. He looked down at his phone:

Can't wait to see you at the party.

Saadiq appeared up on stage as he leaned down to Dray. "Mr. Royce, we have a situation."

"What's the matter?" Dray asked as he stared at him with concern as everyone still gave Chief a standing ovation.

"I've been told that some former employees of yours are still trying to get in here and are making threats."

Clayton and Mayson looked at Saadiq, and then at Dray.

"What's going on, son?" Clayton asked as he and the others still clapped for Chief.

Dray looked at Saadiq as he still did the same. "Handle it."

"Yes, Mr. Royce," Saadiq said, and started relaying information on his headset to the front door of Grayson's.

Several minutes later, this year's summit was cut short and all of the attendees were escorted out of the room and out a private back exit where no media were present.

HOT COFFEE, TEA, AND JUST ME
SUMMIT'S GOING ON!
BLACK BILLIONAIRE MEN'S INVITATIONAL BUSI-
NESS SUMMIT ABRUPTLY CUT SHORT
THREATS MADE TO ATTENDEES, PARTICULARLY,
THE ROYCE MEN

"Hey, everyone, and welcome to my show, I'm Nika Rose, the only one you'll ever need for all of your epic hot coffee and tea, and the pots are hot once again, and what I just got in is very interesting! My source just informed me that the bougie annual Black Billionaire Men's Invitational Business Summit hosted by the Royce men was cut short because of a threat that was made outside of the event or was called in—my source thinks it was both. They also believe that the threats were made by at least two disgruntled former employees of the Royces, and people believe at this point that they have fired so many people in their past that it could be anyone.

"But it's definitely interesting that newest Black billionaire Chief Smith was the one who gave the keynote speech this year, considering the fact that not too long ago he wanted absolutely nothing to do with the Royces. Yeah, how fast things can change! And you know Dray's slut wife Eve had everything to do with it. I guess anyone would've stayed a client at their company if they had the foresight to see that they were gonna end up becoming one of the richest people in the world, espe-cially as a Black man. Chief knows damn well he still hates Dray and the Royce family, he just did what he had to do to become more wealthier than he already is because at the end of the day it's all about the money, isn't it? And Chief proved it!"

I looked at Dray as we sat up in bed later that night. "So has Saadiq given you any updates about the threats?"

"There's nothing to update, Eve. Everything's okay. There's always someone acting up at one of our events, no big deal. I think you know that by now."

"Well, yes, I do know that by now, but is the party still on?"

"Did we announce that it was off?"

I sighed. "Just asking, Dray."

He shook his head. "I know, baby. Sorry for being a smartass about it. I'm just sick of so much shit going on. I'm very much looking forward to the party and so are all of the other men that attended the summit."

"But Harrison's not even legal to drink, Dray."

"He's still automatically invited since he was at the summit. Man, that young lad is gonna be richer than me before he's thirty!"

I smiled. "He's definitely on his way. I just wish we had more young Black men like him because we definitely need them."

"Most definitely. But I look forward to this party every year and don't worry, baby, we have enough security that's gonna be there since those threats were called in. We can't let some stupid-ass people ruin our plans to party because that's what they want us to do. This is a celebration and honor for Black men who are the best in their business and their level of wealth proves it. No one will be let in without showing proof on their devices that they were invited, and the invitations are as always non-transferable."

"I know, honey." I looked at my phone since there was a text:
Can't wait to see you at the party.

CHAPTER 17

THE CALAMITY

"THE WORLD'S RICHEST BLACK FAMILY! BEAUTIFUL!" A photographer shouted out as cameras lit us up as we stood in front of the backdrop of the Black Billionaire Men's Invitational Business Summit party's logo. We stood next to our husbands and honored them by wearing beautiful Oscar de la Renta light blue dresses, with Lulu looking stunning in a $3,450 kaftan cornflower blue dress; Miriam in an amazing $7,990 one-shoulder drape gown with beautiful crystal hem embellishment; and me in a beautiful $15,000 sky-blue structured puffball high-low hem gown that flowed back to the floor. It was also adorned with gorgeous sparkling crystal vine embellishment on the beige strapless bodice. Miriam said the dress was beautiful, but I know she side-eyed the front part of it since it was a little too short for what she liked for me to wear to formal events. I wore my hair up in a huge bun on the top of my head, and my makeup artist was on her game today with the beautiful way she coordinated my makeup with this dress. Just absolutely perfect. I also wore the $201,000 Van Cleef & Arpels Flowerlace diamond necklace Chief gave me. I wanted him to see that he didn't waste his money.

"Beautiful family indeed. The best ever," Wendell Kenton said with a big smile, who was the creator of the Black Billionaire Men's Invitational Business Summit. He was in his seventies like Clayton and had a high eight-figure net worth. His beautiful wife stood next to Mill, as they, as well as a lot of others, nodded with smiles in agreement.

Several minutes later after all of the picture taking was done, I sat at a table and talked to Mill while I noticed there were more women here than men, even though this was an invite for this year's summit attendees and their wives or significant others. It was clear, as always, that some women who wanted to be in the right place at the right time to have their chance at life's finer opportunities had found their way in. And I couldn't blame them.

"Same party, different event," I said, as I took a look around. But there was something I noticed that I hadn't noticed at all of the other parties in the past. "Mill, there's something different about this party."

"What is it?" she asked, and took a sip of her drink.

"Everyone. And I mean *everyone* here, is Black."

"It's like this at the majority of these parties, Eve."

"When it comes to the women? No, Mill, that's where you're wrong. Of course there's a lot of light-skinned women here, but you can tell they're not racially ambiguous or even bi-racial, it seems."

"Yeah, it is looking that way. I guess there's a first time for everything," she said with a grin, and took another sip of her drink. "This night is special, and of course, as always in Anton Stephens fashion, he says he's gonna invited to the invitational one day. And I think he was jealous of the teen, Harrison Moore. He said, 'How is that boy only 19 years old and makes nine figures from some funky-ass socks?'"

I laughed. "Well, he did. His staggering wealth has been verified and everything. Started the business when he was 16 because of his love for all types of socks, but found a way to keep them from snagging holes in them. Amazing."

"It really is," she said with a smile. "I want my kids to learn from him and he's not that much older than my oldest."

"Harrison will be a great role model for a lot of young Black teens since he's so young himself and especially since he still is a teen himself." I looked over and saw Chief looking right back at me as he was completely surrounded by women. "Excuse me, Mill. Chief and I are staring at each other. I think he notices that I'm wearing the necklace he got me. I'm gonna go talk to him."

"Have fun," she said with a smile, and then took another sip of her drink.

We met each other halfway.

"Hey," I said with a smile as I looked up at him.

"Hello, Eve," he replied with a smile as he looked down at me. "You're wearing my gift. Words cannot express how stunning it looks on you and the way you overall look tonight. The necklace just puts it over the top. You are by far the most beautiful woman here. I hope to find someone like you."

"For your third wife?"

He grinned. "And final one if I ever do get married again. I had to be careful before with the level of wealth I was on. Now I'm in a whole other dimension, Eve, so I have to be even more careful than ever before. It's something different about being a billionaire, especially a Black one."

"And you all are as rare as they come," I said with a smile.

"And there's something good about being rare."

"It is," I replied.

Jeffrey Osborne's "You Should Be Mine" came on.

"Love this old-school song," he said as he smiled at me. "Wanna dance?"

"Sure," I replied with a smile, as I looked around for Dray. I didn't see him, but I locked eyes with Leon as he nodded back with a slight smile.

We walked out to the dance floor and embraced into a slow dance.

"I'm surprised Dray let you wear the necklace."

"He didn't mind at all. He's given me a ton of high jewelry so I don't think I've worn even half of it to events. But with you giving me something so extravagant, I didn't want you to waste $201,000 on a piece of jewelry you gave to a woman who is not your wife but is someone else's. The flowers you sent me were just fine. This was too much, Chief."

"Never," he said with a smile, and slowly pulled me closer to him. I almost felt like he was forgetting for a second that we weren't alone in his home. "You smell so good, Eve, like always."

"Thank you," I replied with a smile. I quickly looked around and saw Dray staring right back at me with that same look he gave me when he saw me lying on the floor butt-naked with Chief. Luckily, the song was coming to an end.

Chief noticed Dray as well as the song came to an end. "Thanks for the dance, Mrs. Royce, and once again for that unforgettable night."

"You're welcome," I replied with an awkward smile, since I felt like people heard him say it since we weren't the only ones on this floor.

We went our separate ways as we walked off the dance floor.

Dray met me right at the edge of the floor. "Remember what I said," he said as he stared down at me with that look that was supposed to scare me into submission.

"It was just a dance, Dray."

"You two were a little too close. *I'm* the only one who's supposed to be that close to you when you dance like that."

I sighed as I looked around as people stared at us, including Chief. "Not here, Dray. I'm going to talk to Mill."

He nodded, and walked off with Auer and three other bodyguards by his side.

I sat back down at the table. I looked at her since she was patting her forehead with a napkin. "Mill? Are you okay?"

"Yeah, I'm fine, Eve. I'm just a little dizzy, I don't know why."

"What do you mean you don't know why? I don't like the way that sounds, Mill. You really never get sick."

"Eve, I'm not sick, okay? Stop freaking out."

"Then what's wrong?"

"I just have a headache and some slight dizziness, that's all. Maybe I'm getting too old and too sensitive to loud music or something."

"Look, you've been my best friend forever. You know you can't fool me about anything. You're not pregnant again, are you?"

"Unless the test I took last week was wrong, I'm not."

I looked around for Anton. "I don't see Anton anywhere. Do you wanna go lay down in my private room? I wanted to tell him about how you're feeling and that I'm taking you to my room, but I don't see him anywhere."

"Yeah, I think that'll be best," she said as she sounded short of breath.

Leon approached us. "Everything all right?"

"No, Leon. Mill isn't feeling well. She never gets sick. Could you help me get her to my private room?"

"Can you walk, Mill?" Leon asked as he had his hands on her shoulders. I could even see it in him how concern he was for her and that he'd never seen her look like this.

"Barely," Mill honestly replied. "I'm really dizzy, you guys." She stood up, and *then collapsed to the floor!*

"MILL!!!!" I screamed!

Leon picked her up off the floor and put her in her chair and tried to give her some water, but she appeared to be completely unconscious.

"DRAY!!!!" I screamed as I frantically looked around as I tried to find Anton . . . .

And screamed when I saw him lying on the floor!

And one by one, people started passing out all over the ballroom!

And the ones who weren't passing out were coughing, throwing up, and foaming at the mouth.

"WHAT THE HELL?!?!?!" I screamed as I felt like I was in a nightmare as Dray ran up to me as I looked around at Clayton and Miriam as they stood and looked in horror at people who were passed out around them, as well as Mayson and Lulu who sat at a table and looked just as confused as to what was going on. I looked over at Chief as he was trying to revive a man who was one of the summit attendees as his wife screamed and cried as she knelt by his side.

"WE GOT A SERIOUS SITUATION, FOLKS! EVERYONE WHO IS STILL WITH US STAY CALM! TRY AND STAY CALM! 911 HAS BEEN CALLED SO HELP IS ON THE WAY," the DJ announced in a panic-stricken voice over the speaker.

I looked at the drinks that were all over the tables as well as some spilled all over the floor as it was obvious that the people who were drinking them had passed out while doing so. I looked over at the bar and noticed how all of the bartenders were gone.

This was an absolute nightmare while people screamed just as much as I did about what the hell was going on. It was clear that everyone who had an alcoholic drink tonight had been poisoned, and I knew without confirming it that this was absolutely no accident.

CHAPTER 18

THE ATTENDEES

Todd walked out to the blinding of flashes from cameras to the front entrance of Grayson's as the media was in numbers that I hadn't seen in years, and I meant in years. It was the most I'd seen since Dray and I met, and this was serious. Nothing like this had ever happened at a party here before, and it was by far one of the worst things to happen.

Wrapped in the warmth of Dray's arm as well as his suit jacket, I stood in my party outfit as we all did, with my makeup smeared all over my face from crying and my dress soaked with tears. But the party was over with the second Mill passed out and everyone around her, and luckily, she was going to be okay as well as Anton, and I was hoping that the others were going to be as well because no one ever could tell who was or wasn't going to make a full recovery.

Todd stood at the podium while the entire Royce family stood behind him with our bodyguards surrounding us as he waited for word to make the official statement on our behalf. Wendell Kenton was also behind us with his wife since he was the creator of this event. "Are you all ready?"

"Yes," Clayton answered somberly for all of us as he held Miriam as she wiped tears from her eyes with a tissue.

Todd nodded and began. "Good evening. I'm Todd Johnson, Royce family spokesperson. Tonight, at the Black Billionaire Men's Invitational Business Summit party held here inside the main ballroom, there was an incident which left a number of the party attendees sick. We have confirmed that every person who received this exclusive invite did in fact show up. We can also confirm that there were a little over a hundred attendees, and a little more than half got sick from the drinks they were served while attending this party. We can also confirm that from several tests that have been done on the glasses of these drinks, that there were low-to-moderate amounts of poison in all of these glasses, but not lethal amounts. With that said, I'm happy to say that there have been no deaths from what happened tonight, and everyone who was affected by the poisonings will make a full recovery. But what we don't know is who did this and why. There has been speculation, but we're not going to get into it right here. Most of the people affected by these poisonings have already been treated inside Grayson's or at the hospital and released."

"CAN WE ASK EVE A QUESTION?" a reporter yelled out.

Todd looked back at me, and then at the Royce men.

"Sure," Clayton said.

I sighed as I walked up to the podium as Dray stood next to me with his right arm still wrapped around me and his suit jacket still draped over my shoulders. "Yes?" I said in a calm voice as cameras lit up a very disheveled version of me. I knew I was gonna be the talk about how I looked for a long time, and I didn't care at all.

"Eve, how is Mill, your best friend, and her husband Anton?" the reporter asked.

"They're fine, and I thank God for it because when I saw her pass out like that, I had no idea what was going on. She was experiencing symptoms and everything of someone who could've been poisoned, but it never crossed my mind. I thought she was just sick, and she rarely gets sick, just like her husband. She was the first one to pass out, and then I noticed others passing out all around me, then I knew something very sinister was going on. I'm just glad my best friend and her husband and all of the attendees of the party who were poisoned have been treated and released, and they will make a full recovery. Mill and Anton are at home with their kids and other family members. I pray for the others to have a speedy full recovery as well."

"Dray, did any of your friends pass out?" another reporter asked.

"No, they didn't," Dray informed them. "They didn't have that much to drink. But they told me they felt some mild symptoms, but fortunately for them they weren't that bad to a point where they passed out from them. But I would like to go on record and say that everyone who went to the hospital or got treated inside our family's establishment had their medical bills paid for by our family."

The reporters nodded with smiles as they still took pictures of us.

"That'll be all. Thank you," Todd said.

We all turned around and walked back up to Grayson's, and left through the private back exit. I knew no one wanted to believe that this was intentional, and what was interesting to me was how no one wanted to elaborate on any suspects. It was clear someone did this or paid someone or some people to do it, and to me those people were the bartenders since I knew I was not seeing things when I'd looked over at the bar and they had all disappeared.

CHAPTER 19

THE THINKS

<u>SIA BIJOO'S TEA FOR YOU</u>
BREAKING NEWS!
AT LEAST 60 PEOPLE POISONED AT BLACK MEN'S
BILLIONAIRE INVITATIONAL BUSINESS SUMMIT
PARTY AT GRAYSON'S
DRAY ROYCE AND FAMILY NOT POISONED
NO SUSPECTS IN CUSTODY

"Hello, everyone, and welcome to my show, I'm Sia Bijoo. As you all have seen from the title, a very serious incident occurred at a lavish business party held tonight for some of the wealthiest Black men and their families, and this is a party that is pretty much held every year. But someone seemed to have been very upset that it went on tonight. From what I have been able to gather, this was more about past disgruntled employees who have been let go by the Royces rather than about the people who attended the party, which was strictly be invitation only. It was also said that everyone who was invited had showed, and more than half out of the little over a hundred people who attended were poisoned after drinking alcoholic drinks. If everyone is wondering and I'm sure you all know by now, Dray and Eve Royce were obviously not drinking any alcohol tonight—neither were Clayton and Miriam Royce nor Mayson and Lulu Royce—and that has been confirmed."

"By who?" Dray asked me, as we sat in bed with him holding Stormy and me holding Layton. We just felt like we really needed our kids right now because this could've happened to us whether we drank alcohol or not.

"I have no idea, Dray. Like I said about her, something is different about her than all of the reporters and gossipers who talk about us. Her information is more accurate than anyone else's. She's right, neither one of us were drinking alcohol, and it was never reported that we were or weren't."

"I know," he said, and turned it back on the video:

"Since this is looking like an attempted murder case as it should be, cops were immediately on the scene at Grayson's as people were being treated there. Some had more serious issues so they had to be taken to the hospital. Mill Stephens, best friend of Eve, and her husband Anton, were some of the victims of this horrific event, but as we all heard at the press conference earlier, they have been treated and released, and Eve confirmed it on their behalf.

"I just want to say that in my humble opinion, this was defi-nitely attempted murder, and I think the first people who should be looked at is the bodyguards who were fired for what happened at Mayson Royce's yacht that one day. If there was anyone who had something to do with it, I believe it was defi-nitely them. I will be keeping updates on this story and will bring them to all of you when they become available."

I looked at Dray. "What do you think?"
He shrugged. "It's very possible, Eve, that Brock and Jose had something to do with this, but we can't prove it. If they did, then they

know how much trouble they're in and I was right to fire them. I mean, my other bodyguards had always reported things to me and some even had it formally in writing about stuff that went on between all of them and everything, but never did I think any of them would go this far and poison our guests at a party because I rightfully fired them —but anything's possible."

"Yeah, you're right, anything's possible. So is Detective Cook and the other cops gonna talk to them?"

"Yeah, they're going to. They have talked to Leon and Auer already, as well as some of the other bodyguards who were on-call for the night, and they're still looking for those bartenders because they were the ones who obviously poisoned the drinks, but I believe they were told to do so, and they definitely could've been told to do so by Brock and Jose, or maybe just one of them, I just don't know. I'm just glad no one died as a result of it because the way people were passing out all around us was like a fuckin' horror movie."

"It's still etched in my mind, Dray. I'm gonna have trouble falling asleep."

"You know I'm here for you, baby. You know I'm always gonna be right by your side."

I smiled as tears welled up in my eyes. "I know, honey." He leaned over and kissed me on my head as I kissed Layton as he slept peacefully in my arms, having no idea what his parents had went through hours before. I looked at my phone and smiled. "Mill's obviously feeling a lot better. She just sent me a link to what that bitch had to say about it, and she wasn't short of words."

He laughed. "She never is!"

<u>HOT COFFEE, TEA, AND JUST ME</u>
BREAKING NEWS!
PARTY OF THE POISONED
ROYCE BUSINESS PARTY ALMOST TURNS DEADLY AS
GUESTS WERE POISONED BY DISGRUNTLED
FORMER EMPLOYEES
DO YOU ALL AGREE?

"Okay, first of all, there is no proof that it was any former disgruntle employees who did this. See how she always tries to make it like she's had everything confirmed from her fake-ass reliable sources?"

"I know, honey. Yeah, it's likely the suspects are former disgruntled employees, but nothing has been confirmed by our family that this is true. The cops are still investigating this case because it's far from closed."

"That's for sure," he replied.

We continued to watch:

"Tonight, as you see, I'm having a nice glass of wine to celebrate what happened at Grayson's tonight," Nika said, and took a sip of her wine . . . and then pretended to pass out. She got up laughing. "Nope, no poison in this glass!" she said, as she continued to laugh so hard as if it was the funniest thing she'd ever said and done. "Hello, everyone, and welcome to the show, as you all know, I'm Nika Rose, the only you'll ever need for all of your epic hot coffee and tea . . . and wine tonight!"

"Yeah, that cheap shit. So cheap that it might as well be poison," Dray said, as he shook his head.

"I hope it goes down the wrong way and she chokes. She has no right mocking what happened tonight. It was by far one of the scariest things that'd happened at our parties and we've had some fucked-up shit that has happened at our parties."

"You can say that again."

But we continued to watch what this bitch had to say:

"Look, everyone. Everyone knows damn well Dray Royce and his family was the target of this, but it's clear the person or people who were responsible for doing this wanted it to look like they were targeting everyone. Everyone knows what happened with Ellesse Rosati, and you know if it wasn't those disgruntled former employees, it was definitely someone from Ellesse's family who had something to do with it. Her boyfriend at the time of her death was Chief Smith, and he was at the party, and strangely, he wasn't affected by the poison, either, and confirmed that he wasn't drinking any alcohol. But it's clear that since he's the newest Black billionaire, he's completely moved on very fast from the death of his former girlfriend, but tried to act as if he was still in mourning since he didn't have a date at the party. There is a lot to think about as to who could've done this, that's for sure, so stayed tuned because what I think about this is what everyone is also thinking—whoever did this, Dray Royce is the cause of it!"

"And how am I the cause of it? What the fuck did I do to make someone or some people—because yes, I believe it was the bartenders who put the poison in people's drinks since they were the ones making the drinks—put poison in people's drinks? Anything non-alcoholic such as water or any other drinks that they have to open, they have to let the guest open them, except bottled beer, of course, which they open in front of the customer and hand directly to them immediately after opening them. I saw Chief with a bottle of beer, so you know this bitch is lying about him not drinking any alcohol. I think it was his choice of drink as to why he wasn't poisoned."

"I think so, too. Most people there got specialty drinks like they always do so they have to be specially made. They were everywhere. Mill always gets a specialty drink, so does Anton. But I just have a feeling that not only were you a target there, Dray, I have a feeling we all were—everyone at the party. I just can't explain it."

"Well, I'm not the cause of what happened. And I believe you, Eve, when you say that everyone was a target at that party—but why?"

"That's what we need to find out."

"And we will."

CHAPTER 20
THE OUTCOME

Detective Bruce Cook walked up the driveway of an old, small one-story home while the rain came down at a hard, steady pace. He acknowledged the cop standing at the door and walked in. He sighed as he shook his head.

"Are they the ones you wanted to question in the poisonings at the Royce party at Grayson's?" another cop asked.

"You got their ID's?" Cook asked.

"Right here, sir," a female cop said.

Cook took the ID's from her and looked closely at each of the individuals of interest. "Yeah, this is them," he said, as he stared at Jose and Brock as they sat on the couch along with Lupe . . . .

As they were all dead from drug overdoses.

"We walked in here and found the daughter of Jose and Lupe crawling on both of them. Apparently when we came in, she was trying to wake them up," another cop said.

Cook shook his head in disgust as he looked at everything that was on the table as drug paraphernalia and boxes of pizza were everywhere, and there was still a needle lodged in one of Lupe's arms. The black screen on the TV displayed the message of inactivity. "How long have they been dead because I can see some signs of decomposition already."

"The coroner estimated for a few days," the female cop replied.

"Where is the child?" Cook asked.

"Lupe's parents came to pick her up. They were the ones who called us because they couldn't get in touch with them, so they met us here," another cop replied. "So these were the former bodyguards of Dray Royce, huh? The one's who were fired by him for allegedly putting that girl Ellesse in Mayson Royce's yacht?"

"Yeah, this was them. But it's clear if they've been dead for a few days then there's no way they had anything to do with the poisonings of the guests at the Royce party just a few days later. Damn. Now we're back where we started," Detective Cook said.

"Dray," I said, as I walked up to him while he stood in his office staring out of his window. I noticed he had a small drink in his hand.

He continued to stare out the window. "I suppose I'm the cause of this, too. Right?"

I sighed. "Dray. You had no idea that this was gonna happen. No one knew. It was clear that they were probably doing stuff like this when they worked for you."

"Well, they hid it well and I don't know how they did it if they did because they were all randomly drug tested a million times when working for me and they always came back clean because they knew— as well as all of them—that they were fired if they came back positive for any illegal drugs. I don't play that shit. And when they were tested, it was always witnessed. No exceptions."

"I believe you, Dray. But this is not your fault. You are not the cause of this, so I don't wanna hear you say that again. This is just an unfortunate situation. When you fire someone, you don't know what they're capable of doing because of it—but you're not responsible for it. They were adults who knew what they were doing and knew the risks of doing what they did. You had nothing to do with it." I looked down at my phone. "Mill just sent me some links to people's videos about this. Are you okay to watch them?"

Back in bed in our bedroom, we looked at the first link Mill had sent to me:

SIA BIJOO'S TEA FOR YOU
BREAKING NEWS
FORMER DRAY ROYCE TOP BODYGUARDS JOSE AND
BROCK FOUND DEAD ALONG WITH JOSE'S GIRL-
FRIEND LUPE INSIDE THEIR HOME
CAUSE OF DEATH: DRUG OVERDOSE

"Hello, everyone, and thank you for joining me for this Breaking News, I'm Sia Bijoo. Unfortunately, this is not good news at all, and it was something I'm sure no one was expecting, but I feel to me it's not surprising. Anyone who lands a job with the Royce family has to be some of the luckiest employees because they definitely treat their employees like the royal Black family they are, but when an employee is fired, it's a whole other story. The royal perks are gone in an instant, and that is unfortunately what happened when Jose Lopez and Brock Lebowski—longtime personal top bodyguards of billionaire Dray Royce, were let go by him for their role in putting Ellesse Rosati in Dray's grandfather's yacht. No one ever knew why they did what they did because Dray never told them to do it, and I personally believe him. It also should be believed that once you quit or get fired as a Royce employee, it's very difficult to get another job anywhere because of their connections. It has been said that Dray was not going to rehire them under any circumstances, so that wiped out all hope that they would once again return to that beautiful 8,000 square-foot palace they called home for more than ten years.

"There was great speculation that they were the ones who paid the bartenders at the party to poison the guests and even showed up the day before at the actual summit wanting to talk to Dray, and Dray was notified while the event was going on, but Saadiq, Royce Security Operations Executive Manager,

confirmed that the ones who showed up that day were not
Brock and Jose."

"You know, Saadiq never told me who showed up or not that day he told me that there was a situation while Chief was giving the keynote speech."

"He didn't?" I asked.

"No, he never did, and I admit that I never asked because I assumed it was them—but it was weird because I didn't care that it was them, but I didn't think it was them for sure. He told me about ten people were standing out there wanting to talk to me and my dad and my gramps."

"Well, it was clear it wasn't them, Dray. I think we need to find out who they all were."

"Yeah, eventually."

We continued to watch:

"The coroner said that they had all been dead for a few days, so they were confirmed dead before the party took place. I too believe they had nothing to do with the poisonings at the party, but someone did. As of right now, the bartenders who were ordered to poison the Royce party guests have not been found."

"How does she know for sure that the bartenders were ordered to do this? And by who if they were? Like I told you, Eve, something is different about her."

"Yeah, I'm pretty much convinced of it, too." I looked at my phone. "Well, the other one needs no introduction."

"And if she says something offensive I'm gonna introduce her to my fist."

"Dray. Are you sure you wanna watch it?"

"Turn it on."

<u>HOT COFFEE, TEA, AND JUST ME</u>
BREAKING NEWS!
THE BODIES OF THE GUARDS

TWO OF DRAY ROYCE'S FORMER TOP BODYGUARDS
FOUND DEAD IN ONE OF THEIR HOMES ALONG
WITH GIRLFRIEND FROM DRUG OVERDOSES
CAUSE OF DEATH AND EFFECT: DRAY ROYCE

I looked at Dray as I put it on PAUSE. "Are you sure you wanna keep watching?"
He balled his right hand up in a fist. "Yeah."
"Dray. Undo that fist or forget it."
He grinned and actually listened to me. "Turn it back on."

Nika took a sip of her tea, and then took a sip of her coffee.
"Now you all know that I rarely double fist on the caffeine, but
you know why I'm doing it. Call it instinct, but I had a feeling
that things were not gonna end well with those former bodyguards of Dray's, and my source told me that despite their
pleading and begging to keep their jobs, Dray said, 'No way!
Fuck you, motherfuckers!'"

"I did not say that, Eve, and you know it. I kept it strictly professional with them. Saadiq was there and can confirm everything that
happened."
"Dray, you know I believe you. This bitch just likes to embellish
shit because she knows her subscribers love it. I don't think they
believe what she's saying more than half the time, either."
"Yeah, they probably don't. But it's clear they like her more than
they like us."
"Well, that's haters for you."
"Exactly, baby."
We continued to watch:

"Welcome to this Breaking News show, everyone, I'm Nika
Rose, the only one you'll ever need for all of your epic hot
coffee and tea, and the pots are almost steaming off of the table!
Two of Dray Royce's top former bodyguards, Brock Lebowski
and Jose Lopez, were found dead on a couch in Jose's home

along with Jose's girlfriend, Lupe. The cops said the house was a mess and Jose and Lupe's daughter was all over the place when they got there. Now, everyone, when someone's house is a mess, it's clear that shows a sign of depression. Those guys lived better than most people did, and it's been said that Brock's home didn't look any better, the one he had to move back into with his girlfriend Emily after moving out of an 8,000 square-foot home, a home Jose and Brock lived in with Auer for ten years. No one will ever recover after that, that's a fact.

"I honestly believe that Dray told them to put Ellesse in his grandfather's yacht because he didn't want her in his, but then he double-crossed them and told everyone he had nothing to do with it all the while letting them take the full blame for it, just like what he did when it came to having his baby mama Angela killed. There is nothing anyone can say to me that will convince me that he is completely innocent in Angela's murder. Brittney must have been promised something from him by taking the blame, and to this day, she's still keeping quiet about it. Dray is an evil, sneaky man, and I believe he is responsible for why his two bodyguards ended up overdosing on that shit. They knew they were done, and Dray was gonna make sure of it and he did. Anyone who applies to work as a bodyguard for him or anyone in their family is a complete fool, because you never know what he might end up setting you up for and then firing you over it to make himself look good as if he did the right thing when those guys were only doing what they were told to do by him. Dray Royce is the cause of this, everyone, and doesn't care whose lives he ruins as long as it's not anyone in his family. You all who still work for him better question your loyalty."

"Eve. I hope you don't believe anything this bitch says. She's just trying to ruin my rep and the Royce family rep. People apply to work for us every day. Every day. No matter if it's at Royce Investments, Grayson's, or the private family positions. We have had thousands of applications for bodyguards coming in since it was announced that I fired them. Everyone wants a chance to work for us, and those who are highly qualified to do so will be in consideration."

"I know, honey, and you know I don't believe anything that bitch says. She's literally making a living off of talking about us and sadly, people love it. She rarely talks about anything else. What's worse is that people like the fact that she talks bad about us rather than good."

"People are fucked-up haters, Eve. They know they'll never be in the position we're in just like her, that's why." He looked at his phone. "Get dressed!"

"What?" I said, as I jumped out of bed.

He got on his phone. "Carmella, I need you to bring Stormy up here right now because I need you to watch Layton. Right now. Bye."

"What's going on, Dray?"

"That was Detective Cook. He just texted me and told me that they have one of the bartenders at the station."

CHAPTER 21

THE SERVERS

"State your name," Detective Cook said.

"Brooke Hedley," the young woman replied as her right leg shook nervously. She took a shaky sip of her coffee.

"Brooke Hedley," Cook repeated. "So, you were one of the bartenders at the Black Billionaire Men's Invitational Business Summit party. Correct?"

"That's correct," she replied.

"How many other bartenders were there that night?"

"Including me? There were five of us."

"Five of you," he said. "Okay, so, did you serve anyone noticeable to you?"

"Yes, I served Chief Smith," she replied.

"And what did he have to drink?"

"A bottle of beer."

"Did you open the bottle for him?"

"Yes, because that's what we were told to do. Once we open it, we have to give it directly to the customer, and that's what I did. He said thank you and gave me a fabulous tip even though the drinks were complimentary."

"How much did he give you?"

"$1,000," she replied with a smile.

"Damn! I'm in the wrong business!"

She let out a nervous laugh and took another shaky sip of her coffee.

"Well, Brooke, we know why you're here, and fortunately, if Chief had just that bottle of beer or several other drinks, he was obviously not poisoned that night like how over sixty other people were. Care to tell us who was responsible?"

She sighed. "I didn't poison anyone, sir."

"I didn't say you did, but there's a reason why you're here, Brooke. I think you're here because you know who did and you're feeling guilty about it weighing on your conscience. Right?"

She sighed once again. "That's right."

"So, you know exactly who did this, or let's say, made you and the others do it."

"I didn't do it, sir. I admit that I was told to do it."

"By who?"

"I . . . I don't wanna get in trouble."

"Well, you're here, aren't you? And you're here because you wanna come clean about something, Brooke. You were there. You were there behind that bar serving drinks to a party of some of the most affluent Black people in the world in an establishment owned by the world's richest Black family. Let me ask you something."

"What is it?"

"Was that the first time you worked as a bartender at one of their parties?"

"Yes."

"Because I know it's a very strict process for anyone to get a job there, even if it's just for one night."

She nodded, and took another sip of her coffee.

He sat back in his chair. "Well, I'm listening. It was clear something is definitely going on when it comes to a connection with the bartenders and what happened. Where did you all run off to when you all saw people passing out everywhere?"

She sighed. "We just left out the back employees' entrance and exit. I got so sick I threw up in one of the other bartender's car. He told me the job was done and we were paid to do a job and we did it."

"Wait! *Paid* to do a job? So I'm assuming it was not the bartending job since you were all paid by Grayson's to do that."

"Exactly. He—"

"Who's he?"

"Marchaud."

"Marchaud what?"

"Marchaud Decker."

"And who did he say made y'all do this job?"

She lowered her head.

"Brooke, look at me. Whoever told y'all to do this is in big trouble. They are looking at numerous charges of assault, quite possibly attempted murder, and the Royce family actually wants attempted murder charges brought against you all—"

"I didn't poison anyone!"

"Calm down, okay? I'm just trying to get at the truth here. You need to tell me what was told to Marchaud because I already have someone looking him up right now and we will be sending someone to his house to question him and bring him in here, as well as the other three. Right now, you need to be thinking about how this looks on you, Brooke. You were one of the five bartenders who were serving the drinks. Over 60 people got sick. How do I know you're not lying about being one who didn't poison any one of them?"

She sighed once again. "Because I still have the bag of poison. I never opened it." She pulled out a small bag that had a large amount of a white powdery substance in it.

Cook took it from her as he stared at it, and called in another detective to take it for testing. "Wow. Yeah, it looks like you never opened it, but you know we have to keep it as evidence. You know you violated a major employee rule by even bringing it into Grayson's, right?"

"I know I did. But I never put any of that powder in anyone's drinks, *I swear* I didn't. Look, I'm only 26 years old with three children, okay? I can't afford to go to jail for this, that's why I came here to confess."

"Confess, huh? Well, you only gave me one name, Marchaud Decker. Is he the one who gave out the bags of poison?"

"Yeah, he did. But he got them from someone else."

"Who?"

"Am I gonna get in trouble if I tell you who it is? Because this is who Marchaud told me it is."

"Who is it?"

"A man by the name of Lavell Thomas."

"And why would Lavell Thomas give Marchaud and all of you other bartenders that night tiny bags of poison to put in the customers' drinks at the party?"

I looked at Dray as our entire family watched this interrogation. "Do you know who he is?"
"Yeah, I know who he is," Dray replied.
Clayton sighed. "Me too."

I shook my head. I had a feeling now that there was a hell of a lot to this Lavell Thomas than I ever knew, and we were about to find out.

We all continued to watch:

"Was Lavell at the party?" Cook asked.

"No," Brooke replied.

"Why not?"

"Because he wasn't invited."

"Are you serious? He had you all poison the guests at this party because he wasn't invited? Really? Do you know who he was targeting in particular?"

"Well, Marchaud told me he was first and foremost targeting the Royce family, but none of them had any alcoholic drinks; guess that's a Royce family rule when they're all at parties together. But I guess some others were targeted as well."

Cook got on his phone. "Have someone go get Lavell Thomas right now."

CHAPTER 22

THE OUTCAST

"Lavell Thomas. I'm Detective Bruce Cook," he said, as they shook hands.

"What am I doing here?" Lavell asked, as he sat back in his seat in a black suit, white shirt, and black tie on.

"Well, there's a reason, Lavell. We just don't go picking up people and bringing them in unless we have a good enough reason."

"Are you all sure about that?" he asked with his arms crossed.

"Yeah, I'm sure, Lavell. It's clear that the cops found you at a party. But the party that you attended tonight is not why we picked you up."

"Okay, so why was I picked up?"

"You're in here because we wanna know if you were at the Black

Billionaire Men's Invitational Business Summit party almost two weeks ago."

"No, I wasn't there."

"Why not?"

"Something came up," he replied as he looked down at the table.

"Oh, yeah? What?"

"What concern is it to you?" he asked as he tried not to get angry.

Cook shook his head. "Lavell. We have proof that you were not invited to this party; we have the guest list, and everyone who was invited showed up. Apparently, you seemed to have taken it very personal that you in fact weren't invited to this party. And we also found out that you were also very upset that you weren't invited to the summit the day before the party."

"I should've been."

"And why is that?"

"Because I'm a Black man who has a nine-figure net worth like a lot of them who were in attendance, *that's* why! Every time I try to get an invite I'm rejected. The Royces know damn well why. They can stop this shit, but they don't."

"Wow. Well, what is it that they can stop? How come you keep getting rejected for an invite? This does sound confusing as to why you're always being rejected."

He sighed. "You'll have to ask them."

DETECTIVE COOK APPEARED IN THE ROOM WE WERE ALL IN AFTER excusing himself from Lavell. "Okay, can any one of you fill me in on why he claims he keeps getting rejected for an invite to this summit you all have every year?"

"I don't make up the list of men who are invited to this event because this is not my event. But every man who is invited is approved by me, my dad, and my gramps," Dray said.

"He's right," Clayton said.

"Right!" Mayson agreed.

"Okay, but I still don't understand. He's basically blaming you all for why he keeps getting rejected since from what he has told me, he does qualify for an invite each year."

"That may be so, but it's more than that," Clayton said.

"Much more," Mayson said.

"Like I said, this is not our event. The creator of the summit is Wendell Kenton. If there's anyone he should be taking up any issues with, it is him," Dray said.

Everyone nodded in agreement.

"Okay, let me get back in there to see if he'll admit anything to me," Cook said.

Cook sat back in the room minutes later. "So, Lavell, I'm just gonna ask you flat out—did you have those bartenders poison the guests at the Black Billionaire Men's Invitational Business Summit party?"

"None of this had to happen," he said as he looked down at the table.

"What didn't have to happen, Lavell?"

"I belonged there. I'm tired of being made to feel like an outcast; being exiled from my own community because of who I'm married to."

"Okay, hold on. Who are you married to?"

"Kathy."

"And I'm gonna assume that Kathy is not a Black woman?"

"She's not. She's white and I love the fact that she is. We have five beautiful children. I built a great life for us, but just because I'm married to her, my own community turned their backs on me. The summit is something I should be invited to every year as a wealthy Black man. I make great contributions to the Black community, but it's not enough. The Royces know damn well they have the power to stop this ridiculous shit about excluding Black men like me who have non-Black wives."

"So you're not the only one who has been rejected for that reason?"

"No, I'm not. I know several other Black men who deserved invites but never got them. It's not fair, man."

"Yeah, maybe, maybe not, but what's definitely not fair was for you to give tiny bags of poison to a bunch of hardworking bartenders and making them put that poison into the drinks of those guests because you felt like a jilted little boy who wasn't invited to the big men's party. You know you were wrong for what you did, Lavell."

"And they're wrong for not inviting me."

Cook sighed. "And you were wrong for what you did, Lavell. Had those levels of poison in those drinks been any higher it would've been fatal."

"No one died."

"And you're lucky they didn't. You know that's not the way to go about things, man. So, how do you know Marchaud Decker?"

"He's the son of a man who works for me. Marchaud's dad knows nothing about this."

"How much did you pay each bartender?"

"$10,000."

CHAPTER 23

THE RIFT

TODD STOOD AT THE PODIUM OUTSIDE OF OUR HOME AS WE ALL stood behind him. "Good morning, everyone. As you all know, there were several arrests last night in the poisonings of the guests at the Black Billionaire Men's Invitational Business Summit party. The main suspect who initiated the incident is Lavell Thomas, a man who did not receive an invite to this year's summit and has not received any in the past years. I want to make clear that this summit is for the empowerment of Black business owners and for the growth of their businesses as well as for their Black families. The Royce family believes in keeping what they have built for over a century just like any other family regardless of race. Wendell Kenton, creator of the summit, will like to make a statement."

Wendell walked up to the podium. "Good morning. I'm Attorney Wendell Kenton, I'm also a businessman and creator of the Black Billionaire Men's Invitational Business Summit. This is the only time I am going to make this statement and yes, this is in direct response to the claims Lavell Thomas made last night while being interrogated. This statement will be published on the summit's website and social media pages.

"This summit is for Black men and their families, not interracial families. Interracial families are not Black families. If one non-Black person is a Black person's husband or wife then you're not a Black family, you're an interracial family. Since it's Black men who dominate in these interracial families, then they know what they're doing when they marry and procreate with women of different races. They're building an uncertain future for themselves because his non-Black wife can divorce him and take everything he's worked hard for and go back to her non-Black community with all of it, including their children who will probably grow up and marry, procreate, and build with anyone but a Black person, therefore wiping out everything this Black man worked hard for and built. There's nothing wrong with keeping Black businesses Black. No one will ever know how many businesses started out as Black businesses but ended up owned by people of other races all because of a Black man's choice on who he married, procreated, and built with, and, even worse, sold out to. Let them have their own stuff. They don't have to always be a part of ours. It's been time we separated from interracial families. The Black man made his choice in these cases, let him live with it."

"So, what did you think about what Wendell said?" I asked Dray, as we had lunch together in the kitchen with Layton and Stormy.

"What am I supposed to think about it, Eve?"

"I don't know. You haven't talked much about it since he made the statement."

"And that was his statement, not mine."

I sighed. "Come on, Dray. I know you have thoughts about it and I wanna hear them. Mill will be over here when she gets off of work. She saw the statement live. The incident directly impacted her and Anton and they had nothing to do with it. I personally think Lavell is selfish. I agree with Wendell saying that he made his choice in who he married and he has to live with it. He should've known he wasn't gonna be welcomed into everything when it came to his people."

"Sounds like you have an interesting opinion on this," he said with a grin, and took a sip of his water.

"Well, I do, and I think everyone should have some say about it. I think Wendell just stated what a lot of people are thinking. It's his summit since he created it, so it's his rules. People have to realize that you and your dad and gramps don't always hold the power in everything."

"You're right, we don't. And we don't try and take over other people's businesses or events or anything like that. We create what's ours and we wanna keep what's ours. Goodness, Eve. I can't tell you how many non-Black people wanted to buy Royce Investments in the years we've been open."

"I definitely believe that, Dray. You've told me that a lot since the day we met. And what would this family have if you all would've let them? It is all about keeping what's yours and never selling out. It's too bad Lavell feels like an outcast from the Black community, but I'm sure he's been welcomed to a lot of Black events, but he seemed to have taken not getting invites to this one very personal."

"That's because he does, Eve. I mean, what Black man wouldn't? It's the most prestigious Black event to get an invite to. But hey, it's Wendell's rules, not the Royce men. The event and party are just held at our establishment every year because we're the only Black family in the world who has these things in place and that's because we kept what's ours and never sold out to anyone."

"And I'm glad to be a part of it, Dray," I said with a smile.

CHAPTER 24

THE PUZZLE

"I've never seen a puzzle that expensive in person," Mill said, and then took a sip of her tea out of her Herend teacup as she stared in amazement as I held a piece from my $5,260 PAR 1500-piece "Overflowing" puzzle which featured a vase in the shape of a teapot with overflowing flowers in it.

"Well, as they say, PAR is the Rolls-Royce of puzzles."

"That it is!" she said with a laugh. "I'm afraid to touch it."

"Why? It's just a puzzle. Besides, you helped me with the 'Spill the Tea' 500-piece puzzle. That one was $1,500."

"It was?" she asked with a grin. "You and these expensive puzzles. I guess I'm used to ones you get at the toy stores or on Amazon for my kids."

I laughed. "Yeah, I remember my parents getting me those at the toy stores, too. Never did I ever think I was gonna be able to afford ones that are this pricy. But puzzles are definitely a rediscovered childhood hobby of mine. It helps me relax and unwind. We all have to have our things, you know. If they get too difficult, I just stop doing it because it's supposed to be relaxing."

"You're right, it is. But speaking about puzzles, that Lavell sure has a lot of pieces missing from his brain."

I grinned. "And why is that, Mill?"

"It's just that I don't understand for the life of me why he thinks that he should always get an invite to the summit. I mean, what he did personally affected me and Anton, as well as many others. Anton told me that he has a colleague that knows who Lavell is, and he said that he was the type who was always bragging about his wife being white and that he wouldn't have it any other way and that he couldn't stand the majority of Black people."

"Interesting. So interesting that if he couldn't stand the majority of his own people then why did he want an invite to the summit?"

"Because it was just that, a prestigious Black event. He's the type who acts like he's always entitled to Black events even though he's not with a Black woman. No, boo, it doesn't work that way, and good for Wendell for making that clear."

"Yeah, Wendell is very pro-Black. And like Dray said, it's his summit so he has every right to be the way he is about how he runs it and who he invites to it. I have to agree that these Black men make a choice in who they marry and procreate with, so they can't get upset if they're not included in certain Black events, especially business ones."

"And don't you notice that a lot of these Black men who are with non-Black women don't even bring them to Black events? But they'll take them to non-Black events all the time?"

"Yeah, they do that a lot. Personally, if your wife or husband—because Black women are marrying a lot outside of their race as well now—is uncomfortable in the presence of your people, then that's a problem."

"It most definitely is, Eve. And men like Lavell are all-too eager to go to non-Black events showing off their non-Black spouse as if he fits in with them—yeah, in his damn dreams. And they try and do it at Black events even more and think we Black women should be hating off of them, as if they have some sort of prize."

"No hater here."

"Me neither. And what's so puzzling to me is why men like Lavell feel like they have to go out of their community to find love, but get upset when they're excluded from events in their community. That's the chance they take from their choices. Wendell's statement today needs to be put up on a wall with lights shining on it."

"I'm sure a lot of pro-Black people will agree with that!"

Mill smiled as she looked at her phone. "I just got a notification that Sia Bijoo has something to say about Lavell's arrest."

"Turn it on."

SIA BIJOO'S TEA FOR YOU
ARRESTS MADE IN ROYCE PARTY POISONINGS AT GRAYSON'S
WEALTHY BUSINESS EXECUTIVE LAVELL THOMAS MASTERMIND BEHIND IT ALL
"I SHOULD'VE BEEN INVITED"

"There has been an arrest made in the poisonings that happened at the Black Billionaire Men's Invitational Business Summit party at Grayson's that left over 60 people sick. Wealthy Black businessman Lavell Thomas, who boasts a net worth in the nine figures, says that he has been rejected for an invite to the summit every year and now found out the reason for this happening by way of the summit's creator Wendell Kenton's statement. Lavell stated to Detective Cook that he paid five bartenders $10,000 each to put poison in the drinking glasses of the guests at the party. His main target was the Royce family because he felt they could've had more of a say in him getting an invite, but the Royce men said they don't have anything to do with who gets invited and who doesn't.

"But I personally agree with Wendell in the fact that Lavell should've made a better decision about who he decided to show his allegiance to when it came to marriage and procreating and building. You're not promised anything because you think you should be. This man is well accomplished, but you can't have your way with everything. He's set to be arraigned in a few days."

"Yeah, that's really funny coming from her when it comes to her agreeing with Wendell because this chick looks racially ambiguous as hell," Mill said, and took another sip of her tea.

"She does. But she probably identifies as a Black woman. A lot of them do. But what I wanna know is how the hell did she know about Lavell giving those bartenders $10,000 to put the poison in the glasses? That information was not released to the public."

"Really?"

"Yeah, it wasn't. We all heard him say this for the first time while we watched Cook interrogating him, but the cops did not release it to the media."

"Maybe she has a connection to the cops."

"It's possible. But I think her connection is coming from some-place else."

"Where?"

"When I find out, I'll tell you."

CHAPTER 25

THE TOKENS

"Now you all know I love you all and appreciate you all. I don't take my men for granted who put their lives on the line every day to protect me and my family. I also know when you all haven't been yourselves, and that is perfectly understandable because it's all a part of being human. We all have feelings. I can't remember the last time I did this for you all, and given what'd happen with two of y'alls former colleagues and friends, I felt that this was just the right time to do it again. So, without further ado, here are some tokens of my appreciation to all of you for the wonderful job y'all do," Dray said.

Dray's bodyguards smiled big in anticipation for the gifts they'd received from him since he'd rarely thrown them a party in their honor, and especially here in one of the private party rooms at Grayson's. I had the gifts beautifully wrapped because I also wanted to show my appreciation for them as well. But this was Dray's thing. He was the one who was a born-in Royce, so he was the one who was in charge of most of the personal family business employees such as the bodyguards, and I was glad to be witnessing this type of party since it was the first time that I had. It was a super casual party, so I decided to rock my Louis Vuitton $2,440 LV X YK Painted Dots Nano Speedy along with a pair of Louis Vuitton $1,080 Time Out sneakers. I

129

completed my look with a plain white Majestic Filatures short-sleeved cotton tee and Mother slim-cut ankle skinny jeans

"My baby will hand you all your gifts now," Dray said with a smile, and took a sip of his energy drink.

I smiled as I took one of the bags off of the beautifully decorated table with one of the bodyguard's names on it and handed it to him. And one by one, I did the same for all of them.

"Y'all can open them as soon as she hands them to you. No need to wait until everyone gets theirs," Dray said with a smile.

And that was all he had to say when they all started hollering in pure joy and excitement at the extravagant gifts they'd received from Dray—a pair of Louis Vuitton "Nike Air Force 1" by Virgil Abloh sneakers of their choice which were priced between $2,750 and $3,450; along with their choice of a Patek Philippe watch. Dray told me that they were told to send him their Wish Lists of what they wanted, and the overwhelming majority of them wanted items from these designers.

I noticed how there was a bag missing.

"Where's mine?" Leon asked Dray with a smile.

I looked at Dray.

"You don't get anything," Dray replied in a cold manner.

I gasped as I looked at Dray. I thought he was kidding. But the look he gave Leon told me he was dead serious. "Dray! Come on, stop kidding," I decided to say anyway.

"Does it look like I'm kidding?" Dray asked as he stared coldly at me as well, and then fixed his glare back on Leon.

"What? Are you serious, man? Why not? How come everyone else got something and I didn't, man? What did I do? Come on, now," Leon said, as he tried to laugh it off. But I could see it all in his eyes that he was very embarrassed and humiliated by Dray's decision not to give him a gift like how he gave all the rest of them, and I wanted to know why just as much as he did.

The party suddenly turned very cold as everyone was now looking at Leon standing in front of Dray as he still thought this was a joke that everyone was in on, including me.

"You know why you didn't get anything, man," Dray said.

"No, I honestly don't know why, Dray, so tell me," Leon said as he stared at him with an extremely disappointed look on his face. I could tell that Dray really embarrassed the shit out of him with doing this, and I couldn't blame him.

"I don't know why, either, Dray. How come he didn't get anything, huh?" I asked.

Everyone stared at Dray waiting for him to answer.

Tension became so thick in this room it was almost hard to breathe.

"He's gotten everything, amongst other things," Dray said, as he reciprocated the same look Leon had on him. I didn't want the two of them to get the fighting up in here. "Besides, you can afford to get what I got everyone in here many times over, man."

"That's not the point, Dray, and you know it!" I said, as I tried very hard not to get mad, because now he was being ridiculous and selfish. This obviously went deeper than Leon getting the reward money from him; this was definitely about our ongoing affair, and definitely about something else as well—I just didn't know what it was.

Leon nodded with a stern look. "I don't know what the hell you're talking about, but cool, man. Cool."

Dray gave him a smug look in return. "Yeah, I wish I could say the same."

"Dray!" I said. I looked at Leon; words could not describe the look on his face as he stared back at me. Dray had caused irreparable embarrassment to someone who was so committed to working for us. I honestly didn't know how I was gonna make this up to him.

Mill approached me. "Whoa! I didn't think I was gonna see anything like that at this party!"

"Yeah, neither did I," I said, as I watched Leon smile as Auer uncomfortably showed him his sneakers and watch. "I don't know what Dray's problem is as to why he did what he did. I know he didn't wanna say it about us having an ongoing affair that everyone knows about, but it's got to be something else that he's not telling me."

"Something that obviously has to do with Leon."

"Yeah, it definitely has to do with him. He really took me by surprise with this, Mill. I never thought he would do something like this. See, he tries to use that reward money as an excuse as to why he didn't get him anything, but that doesn't mean anything. He got that reward money years ago and yes, he became a very rich man because of it and still decided to continue to work for us." I looked over at Dray as he talked to some of his bodyguards as he checked out the gifts he'd gotten them. "Dray knows we're gonna have a nice little chit chat about this when we get home."

"Let me know how it goes."

I nodded as I looked over at Leon as I saw him shake hands with one of the other bodyguards and walked towards the door and out of the room. I looked around as Dray was still talking to the other bodyguards as he laughed and sipped on his energy drink as if he didn't do what he did. I walked out of the room and saw Leon headed towards the exit.

"LEON!" I yelled, as I ran to catch up to him.

He kept walking and walked right out of the door as I caught up to him. He stopped and stared down at me.

"Where are you going?" I asked.

"I have no need to be here, Eve."

I sighed as I shook my head. "Leon, I don't know anything about why he decided not to give you a gift, okay? What is going on? Is there something you're not telling me? Dray wouldn't do this for no reason."

He shook his head as he looked over me. He stared down at me. "Dray Royce is just being Dray Royce. I don't think he's ever liked me, Eve, even before we started our affair."

"Leon, I'm just as confused as you are about why he did this. And I'm so sorry you don't think he's ever liked you, but I just don't think that's a hundred percent true. If he didn't like you I don't think he would've ever hired you to begin with and especially hired you to personally protect me and now Layton. And I especially don't think he would've given you that reward money for rescuing me and Layton from those kidnappers that day. He would've found an excuse not to give it to you, especially when you announced that you didn't want it."

He continued to stare at me. It was like he wasn't listening to a word I was saying. Something was seriously going on. Dray had really done it this time. I felt like I wasn't getting through to someone I felt so close to and could always talk to about anything no matter what.

"Look, I can get you those gifts that the other bodyguards got. You know I appreciate you a billion percent and beyond."

"This is not about the gifts, Eve. This is about him disrespecting me a million times over, and I just can't take any more of it even though I thought I could. My mental health is deteriorating because of it along with other things as well. I'm glad he gave me a second chance at my job, but everything has just gotten too much for me to handle."

Tears welled up in my eyes. I could not believe he was saying this; I never thought he would say this.

"Leon, please. Don't. *Don't* leave me. *You said* Dray and I had a bodyguard for life when he gave you the reward money. You have a hell of a lot of life left and you know it. You said that. You. Said. That."

He stared down at me. "I know what I said, Eve. I remember it clearly. But things just haven't gotten better, and you know you can't deny that. I'm just sick of all of the bullshit, Eve, and I know I don't have to put up with it. Dray has a serious problem with how he treats people and it's his problem, not mine, and it's definitely not yours. I know our ongoing affair has caused a lot of shit, but Dray has caused the most shit out of everyone."

"Yes, I know, Leon. And I know all-too well how Dray is, and no one can fix him but him. He is the cause of a million things, it seems, but the one thing I don't want him to be the cause of is you leaving me and my family."

He sighed and stared all around me. He stared back down at me. "I need to take care of myself, Eve. You're gonna be okay. You're gonna be okay." He leaned down and kissed me on my forehead.

"LEON!!" I screamed, as he slowly walked away from me and disappeared into the darkness. I collapsed to the ground and cried.

"Eve!" Mill said as she ran up to me and helped me up off the ground. "What's the matter? What's wrong?"

"He left, Mill! Leon left me!"

"Stop joking, Eve."

"I'm not! He literally just left! He couldn't take Dray's shit anymore! I don't have a bodyguard anymore or a great friend!"

"My goodness," Mill said as she shook her head as she held me. "Look, I don't want anyone seeing you like this. I'll drive you home. Anton can get a ride home with one of the other guys, I'm sure he's not gonna mind."

I cried as I looked back to see if Leon would reappear. It was like a bad movie in me seeing someone that I loved and cared so much about just tell me that I was gonna be okay and then just walked away and out of my life. I just didn't have a good feeling about this at all.

THE GONER

<u>HOT COFFEE, TEA, AND JUST ME</u>
LIVE WITH BREAKING NEWS!
LEON LEAVES!
LEON VICAUT, PERSONAL BODYGUARD AND LOVER
OF EVE, LEAVES ROYCE FAMILY AFTER DRAY DOGS
HIM OUT OF OVERPRICED GIFTS AT BODYGUARDS'
PARTY

"Okay, let's all be honest if we can, okay? Okay! Oh my god! Who didn't see this coming? I called this shit a long time ago! I knew that man was gonna end up leaving their family for good because Eve's pussy was not gonna be good enough to make him stay, and there was no reason he was staying anymore and it's all because of Dray! Hello, everyone, and welcome to the show, I'm Nika Rose, the only one you'll ever need for all of your epic hot coffee and tea, and the pots are steaming hot that I have to let them cool off, y'all! I can't even take a sip out of these cups right now because they're so hot! But while I wait until I'm able, here's what I know from my sources. There was a party thrown by Dray for his bodyguards tonight at Grayson's, and this was supposed to be one of the rare times Dray has thrown a party for them, and we know why he did this because he was the cause of what'd happen to two of his former bodyguards—we all know that, too!

"But to make it up to them, he gifted them some overpriced Louis Vuitton Nike sneakers and even more overpriced Patek Philippe watches. But Leon didn't get anything from him, and it was said he didn't because he got that reward money a few years ago, but everyone knows this was definitely about something else, and that something else was standing right at that party as if she was completely innocent. Bullshit. This was a hundred percent about the ongoing affair Leon and Eve are having, and everyone at the party knew it, they just didn't say anything. It was said that Leon left the party and Eve went after him, and then after talking to him, left the party herself in tears with her best friend Mill. Now I don't know for the life of me why this spoiled-ass billionaire bitch was crying over a man she knew damn fuckin' well she is never gonna leave Dray for. She was crying simply because she lost her lover and now has to put up with Dray's shit all of the time instead of running off to Leon and having sex with him after she got into a fight with Dray. Well, bitch, you can't have everything! You wanna stay with a man who has caused more pain than pleasure all because you don't wanna lose your status as a billionaire Royce wife, well, this is what you get! Your lover ain't coming back to protect you or your little spoiled-ass kid—get used to it!

"When Dray fired him that day Eve and Layton went missing, Leon should've taken that as a blessing because everyone knows that Leon should've left a long time ago, especially when he got that reward money. Who the fuck would've stayed after getting that kind of money? Only a fool would've, and Leon was a fool, but now I have more respect for him than I ever thought I would since he woke the fuck up about who he was working for and finally got the hell out! Everyone else would've left skid marks!"

MILL LOOKED AT ME AS TEARS STREAMED FROM MY EYES AS SHE turned off the video. "Are you gonna be okay?"

"No," I honestly replied as I patted my eyes. I took another shaky sip of my hot tea that she made us as I sat on my chaise lounge in my office. "I'm never gonna have another bodyguard like Leon. He's not coming back, Mill. I don't know if I'm ever gonna see him again!" I broke down into a flood of tears.

"Oh, honey," she said, as she embraced me. "I believe you will see him again. I think you just need to give him this time to take care of himself like how he said he has to do. We all have to do it from time to time. It's just a natural human process. You're not human if you don't have feelings, and when they get hurt beyond measure, that's when you know you need to pull yourself together and do what you have to do, and that's exactly what Leon is doing. Whatever he decides to do next in his life, I'm sure you'll support him."

"I need him, Mill. I hate to sound so fuckin' selfish right now, but I do. I never thought I would need someone more than Dray, but I need Leon. There is just something so special about him. I felt a connection with him almost instantly when I first met him, and I knew that connection was real on his first day on his job with me. I knew there would be no one else like him, and I was right. I just never thought he would leave me like this, Mill. I just never thought it."

I continued to cry as she continued to embrace me. Mill was my forever and ever, and she was always the real one. She was beyond a best friend. She was the sister I never had, and we were closer to each other than she was to her own sisters. Just like no one could compare to Leon when it came to the connection we had, no one could compare to Mill. But I just didn't know if I had it with Leon anymore. I didn't even know how he felt about me anymore. I wanted to think that what he did was selfish, but I would've been selfish to think what he did was selfish. He simply did what he had to do, and it's what anyone who cared about themselves would've done.

Mill looked up towards the door, and gave me nudge while she still held me, as that was a sign that she wanted me to look at what she was looking at.

And there Dray stood in the doorway.

"Hey, Dray," Mill said with a slight smile.

"Mill," Dray said, as he looked at me. "I wanna be alone with my wife."

Mill put her arms around my waist. "I'll call you later on, okay?"

"Okay," I replied with a weary smile. I wiped tears from my eyes as she gave me a kiss on my cheek.

"Thanks for bringing her here," Dray said to Mill.

"You're welcome, Dray," Mill said with a smile, and left the room.

Dray grabbed the remote and turned off the TV and walked over to me. I turned away from him while still on my chaise lounge. "I'm not going away, Eve. You know we need to talk about this." He sat on the chaise lounge that Mill always sat on. "I really did it this time, didn't I?"

"You sure did," I said, as I still had my back towards him. "That was one of the most disrespectful things you've ever done, Dray."

"I can think of more disrespectful things, Eve, and it has nothing to do with me."

I turned and looked at him as he stared back at me. "So it was about me and Leon's affair, huh? As if you're not always fucking around on me, Dray, so don't even start that shit."

"Eve, I did what I did for a reason, okay? And it didn't all have to do with you and Leon still having an affair or him getting that reward money."

"Bull," I said, as I stared at the dark screen on the TV.

"Look at me, Eve."

"No."

"Fine, you don't have to. But what you do have to know is what I just told you. This was about something other than the fact that the two of you are still having an affair and it had nothing to do with the reward money despite the fact that everyone thinks those are the reasons."

"Yeah, and whatever it is that you're making up, Dray, it didn't mean you had to embarrass and humiliate him like that in front of his colleagues and friends. You made yourself look like an A1-asshole and you damn well know it. Do you like doing shit like that, Dray? Do you really? Because it doesn't make you look good at all. You made yourself and this family look bad."

"And that's your opinion, Eve. Like I said, I did it for a reason."

"Yeah, whatever. Leave me alone. You would've never done that to Auer; your dad would've never done that George."

"We would do it to anyone who deserved it, Eve."

"Yeah, so much for employee loyalty."

"Yeah, and Leon showed you he wasn't loyal to this family and especially to you and to our son after all, Eve."

"And what the hell did you think he was gonna do, Dray? Be for real! I think anyone would've done what he did! I honestly believe that you're just making up shit about him because you just didn't wanna get him anything because of our involvement with each other as well as him getting that reward money—oh, and the fact that you just flat out don't like him. He even told me he thinks that you've never liked him."

"If I never liked him, Eve, I would've never hired him to begin with, much less rehired him after firing him—and I went back on my own word about that. And I especially would not have given him that reward money after rescuing you and Layton and especially since he said he didn't want it."

"Well, you don't have to rehire him once again because he's gone for good, Dray."

"I didn't fire him, Eve. He walked away. He walked away from you and Layton and the Royce family. My dad and Gramps have been briefed on what happened tonight, and they have left it up to me to make a decision about it."

"About something that you caused, Dray? Really?"

"I'll give him a day or two to calm down since I know he wasn't expecting what had happened at the party and for me to say what I'd said to him at the party, but if he doesn't come back to work or contact me personally after that time frame then he's gone for good."

"HE *IS* GONE FOR GOOD, DRAY! HE'S *NOT* COMING BACK!"

"Stop yelling," he said as he glared at me. "And did he tell you he was leaving for good and not coming back?"

"No," I calmly replied.

"That's all the time I'm giving him."

He got up off the chaise lounge.

"I'm sleeping in one of the guest rooms tonight," I informed him.

He glared down at me as I gave him the same look. "Suit yourself."

I sighed tears welled up in my eyes once again as I tried to call Leon once again for the hundredth time, it seemed.

No answer.

Carmella gave Auer a small glass of hard liquor.

"Thanks," he said as she sat on the couch with him.

"You're welcome," she said as they passively watched TV. "So, that had to have been the most interesting party you went to, huh?"

He shook his head. "Didn't see it coming. None of us did. Just like with Jose and Brock. But fortunately, Leon is still here. I just wish I knew where he went."

"He didn't tell you?" she asked, and took a sip of her own drink.

"No, he didn't say anything to me about leaving when he was at the party. He just told me my gifts were nice and said that he would see me later. Man, I felt so bad showing him something he didn't get himself. I rarely disagree with Dray, but he was wrong to have done that to him."

"He must really hate him," she said, and took another sip of her drink.

"Well, he never told me he does so I don't think he does. Dray just does certain things because he can. I know he's pissed about the ongoing affair Leon and Eve were having, but I didn't know he was gonna do something like this. I mean, it shouldn't be a big deal, but it is. Yeah, sure, Leon could get what we all got from Dray as gifts many times over, but that's not the point. Dray may do things because he can, but what he did to Leon was for a reason, and it was a reason other than the affair and the reward money."

"And he didn't tell you what the reason was when you drove him back here?"

"No, he wouldn't tell me; said he didn't wanna talk about it. The party ended early, obviously, since Eve had left without telling Dray because she was so distraught because Leon just left the party, and I mean, he had every right to leave."

"So you think he's gone for good like what everyone on social media is saying?"

He sighed and took a sip of his drink. "Yeah, he just might be. And if he is, he's not coming back for anyone, not even Eve."

Todd and Kasi stared at each other as they'd just got done watching one of the several videos of Leon leaving the bodyguards' party as well as the Royce family.

"So, I know you have an opinion on this," she said as she raised her eyebrows at him.

"And it has to be private opinion, Kasi, you know that."

"Yeah, I know. So, what is it?"

He shrugged. "I honestly don't know what to think of it. I was briefed on it by Dray about what'd happened since I was not there, but he said that I don't need to give any official statement about it unless it's necessary."

"Unless it's necessary? Interesting. So, what will make it necessary to confirm to the world what everyone knows?"

He smirked at her. "And what does everyone know, Kasi?"

"That Leon did in fact leave. Can't blame the man one single bit. Everyone seems to act as if it's a dream to work for the Royce family, at least you sure as hell did."

"And would you be sitting here in a million-dollar home if it wasn't? Where would we be if I was still on that show talking about them instead of actually working for them? Yes, I believe it is a dream job of mine, but no, it hasn't been a dream all of the time. But I'm living better than I ever have my whole life, and so are you and Christopher. Leon, I'm sure, is living better than he ever has all because of that reward money he got."

"And he was a fool to have stayed working for them. Who does that? Yeah, Eve definitely had some hold over him, and you saw that personally that one day in her private room at Grayson's."

"Stop it."

She shook her head with a smirk. "Well, you witnessed at that party just how well they connected, and he pulled a gun out on you in the process of her letting him personally hit it for the millionth time probably. That man was already losing it, that was clear. But I guess anyone would lose it working for that family."

"*I said* stop it," he said in a terse tone. "I saw something I should not have seen. Eve apologized to me for it."

"Only because she was forced to by Dray. Your words, not mine."

He grinned. "You're never gonna be happy with me working for them, are you?"

She shook her head. "They have hurt so many people, Todd. I just don't see an end to it."

"And so many people have hurt them, too, Kasi. Much more than we would ever know. They're a strong Black family. They would not be where they are today if they weren't. Now I don't know the whole story as to why Dray didn't gift Leon with anything; he said Leon knew why, but no one has heard from him since he left the party. Wherever he is, I just wish him well."

She nodded. "Me too. Because anywhere has got to be better than working for them."

He shook his head as he looked at her, and then turned his attention to his phone. He got out of bed.

"Where are you going?"

"Looks like this is an even bigger story than I thought. I gotta get to Dray's house for a press conference about it."

"Are you serious?"

"Would I have gotten out of bed if I wasn't, Kasi? It's clear that social media has really blown this thing up about Leon being gone, and the Royces wanna make an official statement about it. I'll see you later."

"Fix your face," Dray said as he glared down at me.

"Fuck you," I replied as I stared straight ahead at the media as we stood behind Todd as he got ready to speak at this press conference in front of our home. I was in no mood for this shit and I didn't care how my face looked.

Clayton looked down at me like he couldn't believe I'd said that to his precious son. I was about to say the same thing to him if he objected to it. He knew this was Dray's fault as to why Leon had left, and now I didn't know if I was ever gonna see him again. And I was supposed stand up here and smile as if everything was going to be okay? Yeah, okay.

"Are you all ready?" Todd asked, and then glanced at me.

"Yes, we're ready," Clayton replied for all of us.

Some of the bodyguards who attended the party stood behind us, as well as Saadiq, who was the head of them all. It was only Clayton, Dray, and me that were in attendance from the Royce family standing out here, but they found it to be a big deal that Leon had wandered off and it was the number one story trending on social media, and when anything happened where our family was concerned, we all had to give a press conference about it to set everyone straight.

"Good evening, everyone. Thank you for joining us here for this press conference in regard to Leon Vicaut, bodyguard of Dray and Eve Royce, and Eve and son Layton's personal bodyguard. We want to clear up any speculation as to what went on this evening that has been circulating on social media. We want to first say that Leon is not a missing person. Let me repeat that, he is not a missing person. He attended the party at Grayson's that Dray threw for the bodyguards. He left without telling Dray, and that was the last time anyone had heard from him despite Dray and Eve's, as well as other people's attempts, to contact him. He did not tell anyone where he was going. He has not been back at the house that he shares with three other bodyguards. His parents, who are in France right now, have said they haven't heard from him, either, and are still actively trying to contact him. We'll bring you any updates on his whereabouts as soon as they become available. We're not taking any questions. Thank you."

I stormed off away from Dray as I walked back up to the house by myself as tears welled up in my eyes. I felt that everyone was staring at my back. I even heard my name being called several times as I continued to pretend that I didn't hear a thing as flashes from cameras lit up my backside. No one knew how I was feeling right now; they didn't understand. And it was typical that Dray didn't want Todd to tell the media about why this all happened to begin with because he was naturally the cause of all of it.

CHAPTER 27

THE PROPOSITION

It was a few days later and there was no sign of Leon anywhere. It was like he'd vanished without a trace. No one had seen or heard from him since the night of the party. It was clear to me that he was serious. He said I was gonna be fine and disappeared into the darkness, and I'd felt darkness all over me ever since. I felt like a few days had been a few years since I'd seen him and didn't know at this point if I ever would again.

I came up on passing Dray's office since I was coming from mine.

"EVE! GET IN HERE!"

I stopped in front of his office to find him staring right back at me as he sat at his desk.

"*I said* get in here. You heard me."

I walked into his office and right up to his desk, but I refused to sit down.

He sighed as he shook his head. "How come you cancelled the appearance you were supposed to make this afternoon?"

"Because I didn't feel like going."

He shook his head as he stared at me. "You're only making yourself look bad when you do these things, Eve. You had no reason to cancel that appearance. You're not sick, Layton's not sick or me or anyone in my family or yours. You can't keep doing these things just because you're upset because Leon left."

"And he left because of you."

"Look, I had a long day today, so I don't feel like fighting."

"Neither do I, Dray, okay? I just don't wanna talk to you or anyone or do anything right now."

"Well, you're gonna have to. You have to get used to Leon not being here anymore. I already assigned you a new bodyguard, and he was waiting for you this afternoon and you refused to see him and talk to him or even leave this house. Now you're making me look bad here, Eve. If you don't wanna believe that I had a reason to do what I did at that party then there's nothing I can do about that."

"Stop the bullshit, Dray! You had no reason to do what you did! You just don't like Leon, that's all! He's the only man that would stand up to you and you can't stand that shit and you know it."

He stood up from his desk. "*I said* I had a long day today, Eve. I'm not gonna argue with you. If you miss another scheduled appearance because you're still lovesick over your lover being gone then you're gonna be suspended from your Royce duties. We don't play that shit and you know it." He sat back down as he shook his head. "You want someone back that bad who doesn't wanna come back, huh?"

"He means everything to me."

"Does he now?"

"You know damn well what I mean, Dray."

"I know damn well that I do, that's for damn sure."

"Stop it!" I hissed.

He leaned back in his chair. "Name it."

"Name what?"

"Name it. You know what I mean."

"No, I don't know what you mean, Dray."

He shook his head. "Don't play games with me, Eve. I said I had a long day today. I'm not in the mood for it. It's clear that you're never gonna be the same if I don't do something to get Leon back because you think I'm the cause of him leaving and everything else that's gone wrong since we've met and since we've been married and he's the best bodyguard in the world."

"He is. He's more than that."

"Yeah, I just know he is."

"Stop it, Dray! STOP!"

"Name it," he said again as he glared at me. He got his phone out. "How much you want me to give him to get him back to protecting you again, huh?"

I sighed as I stared up at the ceiling. I glared at him. "Dray. No amount of money is gonna make him come back."

"Bullshit. How much?"

I shook my head. "I just wanna find him and talk to him."

"Anyone can be found, Eve, you know that. It's clear that he's probably not gonna come back unless he's given money to do so. So, how much? I'm not gonna ask you again."

I sighed. "I don't know."

"Well, I sure as hell do. He's a very rich man because of that reward money, so that's not gonna be enough for him this time around. I really did it this time, huh?"

"Dray. You know damn well you're the cause of him leaving. He told me he had to take care of himself, and I could see it in him and hear it in his voice that he was gonna break if he didn't leave."

"How does $300 million sound? Huh?" he asked, as he fiddled with his phone.

"I don't know, Dray, okay? I don't wanna have him think that I forced you to pay him to come back."

"$500 million? And I'll let the two of you fuck each other anytime you want. That should keep him your bodyguard for life no matter how mentally fucked-up he is."

I got up and walked towards the door.

"EVE! COME BACK HERE!" he said as I continued walking. He ran after me and grabbed my arm. "Eve, you know damn well I'll do anything for you. I've always believed in love over loyalty. He showed he wasn't loyal by walking away from us even though he told us he would be with us for life. This is his fault just as much as it is mine, so if there's anyone you should be upset with it should be him as well, not just me."

"Let go of me," I said as I jerked my arm off and away from his hold and walked down the hall as I could feel him staring at my back.

"Yeah, he said he's willing to pay him anything to get him back to protecting me and Layton again," I said to Mill, as she sat with me in my office once again. She decided to come over after work to see how I was.

"I think he's serious, Eve. Dray really loves you and I believe him that he will do anything for you. If paying Leon in upwards of a half of a billion dollars doesn't do it then I don't know what will. Dray won't miss the money at all."

I shook my head. "I just don't want Leon to think that Dray had to do that to get him back. He didn't want the reward money, but Dray gave it to him anyway and that was after he rehired him. I know Leon is not gonna take any money from him; he doesn't need it. I just wanna know where he is and how he is. I miss him."

She gave me a sympathetic smile. "I know you do, Eve. And it's just unfortunate that Dray just doesn't understand how you really feel about Leon. It's clear he really does think he's just a bodyguard to you."

"Well, I think he knows he's a lot more than that to me because he knows I wouldn't be acting the way I am if he wasn't any more than that to me. I cancelled an appearance I committed to going to months ago. Those women were looking forward to seeing me and talking to me. I just didn't feel like going. Everywhere I've gone for appearances I always had Leon right there, staring back at me with his infectious smile as I gave talks, greeted people, whatever it may be. I just can't fathom not seeing him anymore."

"I hope he does come back, Eve, I really do. I believe he is the best bodyguard for you. There are just some people you just instantly connect to, and that was clear it was you and Leon from the start. You could've been stuck with someone who just didn't care as much about you and now Layton as he should've. So, you haven't even met your new bodyguard yet?"

"Not yet. I haven't been out of this house since the press conference. No offense to him or anything, but I'm just not in the mood to meet anyone new."

"Eve. This may be a reality you're gonna have to face. I just want you to be prepared for it."

"I know, Mill, and I'm trying to not think of it as a reality because it very much is for me right now and I don't know if things are gonna be permanently this way for me. I honestly didn't think Leon was gonna do this. I thought he was stronger than this."

"But the strong do weaken, and that's what happened to him."

I sighed. "Yeah, it did. I even conceded that I'm surprised this didn't happen sooner to him. Wherever he is, I just wanna let him know that I still love him and care about him, and I just don't wanna ever lose touch with him if he never does come back." I broke down and cried. She came over and embraced me.

HOT COFFEE, TEA, AND JUST ME
THE PREPOSTEROUS PROPOSITION
DRAY OFFERS RIDICULOUS AMOUNT OF MONEY
FOR LEON TO RETURN TO HIS JOB AS A BODY-
GUARD IN UPWARDS OF $500 MILLION

"Okay, if this is not the most ridiculous shit I have ever heard then I don't know what is. Who the hell would offer to give someone this much money to return to some job that only paid him a microscopic of a damn fraction amount a year compared to this? Yes, folks, Dray Royce has officially lost it!

"Hello, everyone, and welcome to the show, I'm Nika Rose, the only one you'll ever need for all of your epic hot coffee and tea. And this is just on some whole other level shit right here. It's clear that Eve is the one who is behind this and put him up to it because there is no way in the world that if I had even a trillion dollars that I would offer someone that much money to come back to a job like that. It's clear Dray was that bad in the way he treated Leon, and it's also clear that Eve is acting like a stupid little teen girl who wants her little bodyguard boyfriend back because my sources told me that she missed an appearance because he wasn't there to protect her. Bitch, please! First of all, ain't nobody gonna hurt your dumb ass. Second of all, ain't no one worth that kind of money to wanna have back on a job that bad. Dray really fucked up this time because if he's offering this much money for Leon's return, then it was clear that Leon must've told him in these past few days through someone that he was never coming back—and who would? If Leon had any dignity, then it wouldn't be about the money. He would stay away just as he walked away. He abandoned his job and he abandoned Eve—what is it that this bitch can't see?"

HOW MANY WOULD GO BACK TO A JOB AS A ROYCE BODYGUARD AFTER BEING OFFERED THAT KIND OF MONEY?

YES, IT'S ALL ABOUT THE MONEY – 99%
NO, IT'S ALL ABOUT DIGNITY – 1%

"You motherfuckers ain't SHIT!!"

"Yeah, and neither are you, bitch," I said, and turned off the video to continue working on my puzzle in my office. I looked up to Dray standing at my door.

"Eve."

I continued to work on my puzzle.

"Stop pretending you don't hear me. We need to get downstairs into the meeting room."

I looked at him. "What for? Who are we meeting?"

"Someone who wants to talk to us about Leon."

Minutes later, Dray forced me to hold his hand as we walked into the meeting room while our executive housekeeper, Nadine, led the way. This was a room used for interviews that we rarely gave. Wealth showed all over it, and that's the way the Royce family wanted it and had always wanted it. There were two of the finest French provincial sofas facing each other where one or two Royce family members would sit on, and the guest would sit on the other. Tonight, the person who was waiting for us was on the sofa facing the cathedral ceiling-to-floor windows. Even from behind, I had no idea who this was.

"Mr. and Mrs. Royce, Sia Bijoo," Nadine announced with a smile.

What the?

"Nice to meet you, Sia," Dray said with a smile as he shook hands with her.

"Nice to meet you," I replied as I shook her hand as well.

"Very nice to meet the two of you," Sia said with a smile as she stared at Dray.

"Have a seat," Dray said as he still continued to smile at her.

I knew he loved the way this racially-ambiguous-looking chick looked, and this was the first time ever that we had a person who had reported several times on us actually in our home with us. And this must've been something pretty significant that she had about Leon since I knew she had to go through more than a few people to get up in our home to talk to us personally about him.

"Thank you for agreeing to meet with me," she said with a big smile as she just couldn't take her focus off of Dray.

"You're welcome," Dray replied with a nod.

I didn't agree to it, I thought, as I still tried to keep my smile.

"So, tell us what you know about Leon," Dray said.

"Well, first of all, I would like to let you both know that he is okay."

"Where is he?" I blurted out as I tried not to let my smile turn into a cold, hard glare.

"He's with a private mental health specialist. He's one of the best doctors in the world who's been treating mental health before people even knew it was a very serious issue. He's in great hands," she replied with a smile.

Dray looked at me. "Happy?"

I sighed. "Of course. How long is he going to be there?"

"For a few more weeks. He's progressing very well. His doctor says that he's doing much better than expected, and Leon even told me himself after being in there for a few days—since I couldn't talk to him for the first few days he was in there—that he instantly felt better once he got there. It's something he said that he definitely needed to do for a long time."

I looked at Dray; he nodded with a smile.

"Well, Sia, as you know, I did make a proposition for Leon that somehow got to social media."

"I'm aware of it," she acknowledged.

I sighed as I stared around the room as I crossed my arms in front of me.

"Did you discuss it with Leon?" Dray asked.

Sia looked at me since I knew she noticed my body language towards Dray asking her this. "Yes, I discussed it with him," she informed us.

"And what was his response?" Dray asked.

She continued to look at me as if she didn't want to tell us. "He said he doesn't want anything from you, Dray. You've given him enough. He just wants to be respected more."

"That goes both ways."

"Dray!" I said, because I knew why he'd said this.

"I understand, Mr. Royce."

"Dray," he replied with a smile.

She nodded with a smile.

"How were you able to get access to Leon when no one else could?" Dray asked.

I stared at her since I really wanted to know the answer to this myself.

She stared back at me, and then looked at Dray. "We're together."

"Together?" Dray asked. He looked at me, and then turned his attention back to her. "Where did you meet him?"

"At the Sexy Six party," she replied with a smile as she stared at Dray. She was avoiding eye contact with me for a reason.

"Interesting. I didn't see you there," Dray said with a smile.

"Neither did I," I said as I tried not to glare at her, since Leon told me he was not serious about any woman he met there that night.

"I was there. I didn't know him prior to the party," she informed us.

"Has he talked to you about why he left the last party he was at early? You know, the one I threw for the bodyguards?" Dray asked.

"He didn't talk about it that much. He just told me after he'd left there that he was gonna head on out to be treated by the mental health specialist, and that he would talk to me in a few days," she replied.

I looked at Dray. I knew he wanted to see if Leon had told her that he was the reason why he'd left the party early. I felt Leon did tell her exactly what'd happened, she just didn't wanna say anything for fear that she might get Leon in trouble for some reason and jeopardize his chances at working for us again.

"If you're being honest about how private his treatment is, Sia, then it's very interesting that you have a lot of access to him because I know not all people get that with him," Dray said.

I looked at her.

"I am on his approved visitors list."

"Is that all?" Dray asked.

It was like he wanted her to admit something that she didn't want to admit in front of us, and if this was true, I was waiting to hear it.

"No, that's not all, Dray," she replied. She shot a quick glance at me.

"I'm listening," Dray said with a smile.

"I'm his wife," she informed us. She held up her left hand that exposed a 5-carat solitaire diamond ring. "We married yesterday."

Several minutes after Sia had left, Dray came up to me as I was back in my office. "Still want him as your bodyguard?"

CHAPTER 28

THE DISHONORABLE

"As you can all see for yourselves, I am fine. And as it was stated by Mr. Todd Johnson at the press conference while I was away, I was never a missing person. No one ever reported me as a missing person. I would like to thank the Royce family for respecting my privacy while I was away to take care of myself, and I am very much happy to be back on my job as a Royce bodyguard. Thank you," Leon said, and stepped away from the podium.

The flashes from the media's cameras lit Leon up as he stepped back with a smile as he overall seemed genuinely happy to be back working for us, but he knew I had a lot of questions to ask him as well as Dray, who stood next to me as he held Layton.

"Thank you all for attending this press conference this morning," Todd said.

I turned around and walked back up to the house as I held hands with Dray as I adjusted my $1,500 Chanel crystal-strass covered oval sunglasses. Leon, as well as Sia, were right behind us. Once we all got in the house, Dray handed Layton to Carmella as she had Stormy in a double stroller.

"Follow us," Dray said to Leon and Sia as he still held hands with me.

And minutes later, we were all back in the meeting room, with now Leon included.

Dray and I sat on the same couch we sat on the last time we were in here, and Leon and Sia sat across from us. I noticed how she tried to hold his hand; but he refused as he still kept a smile on his face.

"So, you both knew we wanted to talk to the two of you after your press conference, Leon," Dray said.

"Yes. What is this about?" Leon asked.

"It's about the relationship the two of you were secretly in for obviously a while. And it's obvious that it got very serious very fast between the two of you since you both are officially married now," Dray said.

Leon and Sia looked at each other as if they did something wrong.

"Is that okay?" Leon asked, and then looked at me and then back at Dray.

"Sure, it's okay, it's just that y'all took us by surprise by it, that's all. It was okay to be in a relationship, of course, but what's not okay is that you hid it from us, and I had to find out through others, Leon, that you were the one who was giving your now wife information about us while you were secretly seeing her, which prompted her to write and talk publicly about us," Dray informed him.

I looked at Leon as he stared back at me. He truly looked sorry. It was clear that he was Sia's source to us. I honestly didn't know how I felt about him for doing this.

Dray looked at me. "Now you know why I didn't get him anything for that party."

"Please don't talk like I'm not here," Leon said.

"It's my house, man, I can talk how I want," Dray said.

"Dray," I warned, because I could feel the tension building up.

"Dray and Eve, you know I never said anything bad about you all and your family. And, Dray, you're right, it was Leon who gave me the info about your family. But I didn't think there was anything wrong with him telling me things."

"It's a violation of his contract. It's dishonorable and unethical what he did, Sia. I guess he didn't tell you that once someone works for the Royce family—and what I mean is working for our private family, not our company family—that they are automatically a Royce insider whether they want to believe they are or not. Didn't matter if he was secretly seeing you, he had no business telling you anything. *Anything.* I knew something was up when you were on those videos talking about things that only the cops knew about, as well as other things," Dray said.

"I'm sorry, Dray," Sia said.

"I'm not the only one sitting here," he said as he glared at her, and then at Leon.

"I'm sorry, Eve," Sia said.

I nodded and then let out a sigh.

"Leon? Don't you have anything to say to my wife?" Dray said.

I knew he was only calling me his wife because Sia was sitting here, and the fact that she and Leon were married.

"I'm sorry, Eve. My actions were inexcusable, and I'm sorry again; you know I mean it. It won't happen again," Leon said as he looked right into my eyes, and I could see it all in his that he'd meant what he said.

"Thanks for the apology, Leon. I appreciate it," I replied with a smile. I looked down at his left ring finger and noticed his single gold wedding band. It was clear to me now that this marriage really did happen between him and Sia.

"So, with all of that being said, Sia, you need to find another family to talk about because you are no longer able to talk about us. Leon is a rich man so it's clear you don't need to work, but you definitely need to find something else to do besides talking about us all the time like all of these other hyenas out here."

"I understand, Dray," Sia said.

"I hope you do, because there will be consequences for you, too, if you fail to follow the Royce rules like your husband," Dray said.

Leon tried not to glare at Dray. "She understands just as much as I do. Right?"

Sia smiled. "Right."

<u>HOT COFFEE, TEA, AND JUST ME</u>
ROYCE BODYGUARD LEON VICAUT MARRIES ROYCE

GOSSIPER SIA BIJOO WHILE IN MENTAL HEALTH
CARE TREATMENT
LEON'S LOVER EVE NOT HAPPY!
DRAY CALLS RELATIONSHIP "DISHONORABLE TO
ROYCE FAMILY"

"Yeah, he's got a lot of damn nerve! Considering the fact that he
is the number one reason why Leon left to begin with, and no
one wanted to mention that at those bullshit past two press
conferences, especially the one today. Hello, everyone, and
welcome to the show, I'm Nika Rose, the only one you'll ever
need for all of your epic hot coffee and tea. And the pots spilled
all over the place when it was announced that not only did Leon
get help for his mental instability, he also secretly wed Sia Bijoo,
a social media thot who just recently started doing videos about
the Royce family, a family that he stupidly came back to
work for.

"At this point, Leon is just a lost cause. I believe he only
married Sia because he knows now that Eve will never leave
Dray for him, and he's moved on in that aspect, but if the dude
really wanted to move on, he would've moved the fuck on and
would've never came back to that stupid bodyguard job. He had
a stellar career as a USAF pilot, and he gave all of that up to be
disrespected many times over by some funky Black narcissistic
billionaire psycho and his slut wife who can't keep Leon's dick
out her mouth and cunt—yeah, I said what I said because
everyone knows it's true. Dray called a relationship he had no
business controlling as being 'dishonorable to the Royce family.'
Why, Dray? Why? People have a right to be in a relationship
and they have the right to free speech and a right to marry, in
case you didn't know, because it was said that because they were
in a relationship that Leon told Sia a lot of things about the
Royce family so that's why she knew stuff that a lot of us didn't
know. If you were so offended by that then why did you let him
keep his job? You were offering him in upwards of $500 million

to come back to his job, and it's clear that he must've gotten some of that money or even all of it because I just don't believe he would've returned at all. He is a newly married man with a thot wife like Dray, so he was probably paid by Dray to come back after all because it is all about the money, isn't it? 99.9% of you said so on my poll! Money and dishonesty go hand in hand when it comes to them. Looks like it's another win-win situation!"

I turned off the TV as Leon smiled at me. "Enough of that shit."

"It doesn't bother me, Eve. I'm just glad to be back with you and Layton."

I nodded with a smile. I looked down at his left hand and noticed he wasn't wearing his wedding ring. I sighed. "Leon. You can wear your wedding ring when you're with me, okay? You don't have to take it off. I don't think Sia would like it at all if she found out you did that."

He nodded with a smile as he reached into his pocket and slipped it on his finger. "Thank you, Eve. I just didn't know what you would think of all of this, I mean, what you would *really think* of it."

"Well, to be honest, I wish you would've told me you were in fact in a relationship with her, Leon. I thought we knew each other well enough not to be keeping secrets from one another, and admit it, you kept this woman a secret. We had no idea that you were even seeing anyone, much less engaged to her and now married to her. This seems like it happened so fast and it just took all of us by surprise, that's all."

"I know it did, Eve. Like I said before, I didn't know what you would think of me being with her. She makes me happy, and I didn't think I ever would find a woman that would make me happy like the way you have, Eve. But you know us being officially together will never be a reality. I had to accept that and move on to make my own reality if I wanted to be with someone. I actually didn't know I was gonna fall so hard for a woman I met at that party that night; I can't lie, but it happened. And I can't say personally to you how sorry I am that I told her things about you and Dray and the Royce family. I had no business doing that. And yes, that is the only reason why she started doing her little show about the two of you. It's all because of me and I'm sorry."

"Well, you don't have to keep on apologizing for it, Leon. Everything's out in the open now. I'm just glad that you're okay and you're back with us. But did Dray give you any money for coming back?"

"Not a dime," he said with a smile. "Sia was actually begging me to take it—the $500 million, that is—but I told her I'd gotten enough from him with the reward money, plus great investments has made my net worth almost double now. She knows not to bring it up again because I told her not to."

"What does Tina think about you marrying Sia?"

He grinned, and then broke out into a chuckle. "She's mad as hell about it; said I was dishonoring her and our son because I chose to marry someone else instead of her since she's my child's mother. I told her I've never loved her and was not going to do something I knew I would regret later on. It's already enough with her being my child's mom, and Sia knows she's officially a stepmom since she has no kids of her own, but I wanna keep her safe from Tina."

"Well, it's who you got pregnant, Leon," I said, as I looked at my phone. "Did you get my latest schedule?"

"I did," he replied with a smile. "I heard you missed an appearance because I wasn't here."

"Yeah, I did, but it won't happen again," I replied, as I still looked at my phone.

He continued to stare at me. "Are you okay, Eve?"

"Yeah, sure. Why wouldn't I be?"

But I knew he could see right through me. Because of him being married now, it had definitely changed our relationship, especially our personal one.

"Eve. You know I know you like the way Dray and Mill know you. Something is bothering you about all of this. I know it seems like I went away for a month and then came back and I'm now a married man and you didn't even know I was seeing someone. I can't tell you how sorry I am that I didn't tell you back then. I just didn't know how you would've reacted to it and if it would've had an effect on the relationship we have."

"What's done is done, Leon. All we can do now is move forward. And in knowing that, we're gonna have to—"

"No," Leon said.

I gave him a surprised look. "No? You don't even know what I wanna tell you."

"I know what you wanna tell me, Eve, and the answer is no."

I sighed. "What do I wanna tell you, Leon?"

"You want us to end our affair. No, I don't wanna end it."

"You're a married man now, Leon. And I'm a married woman."

"I don't wanna end it, Eve. You mean so much to me. I never had any doubts in my mind about not coming back here. Never in my life could I have walked away from you like that. Never."

"Leon, you're a newly married man. You need to concentrate on your marriage, and I need to concentrate on mine with Dray once again. We're with different people for a reason. I think it would be very dishonorable to our marriages if we both continue this."

"I don't look at it as being dishonorable, Eve. I don't think I'll ever love Sia or any woman the way I love you."

I looked deep into his eyes. I knew his feelings for me still couldn't be denied; and mine couldn't be for him. "You know, when Dray made that $500 million-dollar proposition to me to try and get you back when we thought you'd left for good, he told me that one of the things included in it was that he would let the two of us have sex as much as we wanted."

"Is it too late to accept the proposal?"

I sighed. "Leon."

He lifted up my chin. "I'm serious."

We started kissing.

"I missed you so much, Eve," he said in between kisses.

"I missed you, too," I said as we continued to kiss. "We have to make this quick."

"Quickies are usually the best," he said with a smile as he breathed heavy.

And here we were going at it hard once again but this time in my office right on my chaise lounge. I didn't know whether or not I was ever gonna see him again, much less having sex with him again. And I never even fathomed that I would be having sex with him now that he's a married man. This was the first time that I'd ever had sex with a married man other than my husband. I just didn't know if I could actually continue this since things were a lot different for him now, but it was clear he didn't see it that way at all.

"Well, you certainly gave Leon the best welcome back gift he could ask for!" Mill said, and then took a sip of her drink.

"Don't start, Mill," I said, as I shook my head with a slight grin. "I should not have done that. Like me, he's married now. I don't understand why he married her if he still wants to continue an affair with me. When Sia showed us that they were married by way of her wedding ring, it was like I couldn't believe it. I honestly thought she was kidding, but it's clear that she wasn't. They're really married."

"And I'm sorry, but he was a fool to marry her. Who the hell would marry a woman that he met at that Sexy Six party?"

"Well, they did. And I know that Amanda and Lena know about it since they were the ones who started that list which prompted Dray to wanna throw a party since he was first on that list. But I know they're pissed that one of the single men on the list is married now to a woman he met at that party."

She laughed. "Yeah, they probably are! But Chief is still single and now one of the rare Black billionaires."

"Yeah, he is," I said, and took a sip of my drink.

She stared at me as she took another sip of her drink. "How do you really feel about him, Eve? Because I couldn't believe it when you told me that the two of you had sex again and that Dray practically watched it all this time."

"I like Chief, but I'm not in love with him like the way I'm in love with Dray and the way I love Leon. Dray thinks Chief is in love with me, but I don't think so. He's still a client of Royce Investments and that's all that really that matters to Dray."

"Yeah, I believe you. But giving you that beautiful necklace was on some 'I'm in love' shit!"

I laughed. "Well, he can afford to give a woman anything like that like it's nothing, but I believe it was definitely something. I just felt so dishonored by Dray having to do that again. Dray will do anything for his business, and I can't blame him in a lot of ways because I would not be sitting up here in my own private room in a this Black country club if I wasn't married to Dray and if it wasn't for Royce Investments."

"And in that aspect, Eve, I'm glad you have realized what you have. Since you met Dray and the two of you have been serious about one another, you have never taken your relationship, marriage, and life with him for granted. Any woman could've been in your position and almost was. I'm just glad Dray chose you and he chose you because he saw a good woman and knew you would take being his wife seriously and not show off the life he gave you on social media at every single chance you got, and that's very easy to do."

"Thanks, Mill, and it is. Every day I feel like I'm living in a fantasy world since I've been with him. And I do think about the what if, you know?"

"Like?"

"Like what if I never decided to write him for a chance to date him to become his wife? What if it didn't work out between us after all? What if he decided that he just didn't wanna be with me anymore or me with him?"

"Well, the two of you don't have to worry about that because you both are gonna be together for as long as y'alls parents and his grandparents have been together, and that's anything but dishonorable."

"You're right, Mill," I replied with a smile, as we clicked glasses and continued to watch TV. I was definitely hoping since Leon was back with us that this was definitely a renewed start for all of us.

CHAPTER 29

THE SPOKESMEN

"Thanks for accepting my invitation, man. It's just that we're only the very few men who have had the job we have."

"Had. At least for me," Floyd said, and then then took a sip of his hot tea.

Todd nodded. "Yeah, you're right. And I only have it now because—"

"I was fired, and rightfully so," Floyd filled in. "It's okay, Todd. Like I said, I was rightfully fired by Clayton. I could've gotten Dray killed that day by that madman. It was just a messed up incident, and quite frankly, more and more things just started happening where I just didn't know how much I was gonna be able to take anyway."

"Really?" Todd asked. "Because it seems like it's only been weeks since I've been on the job even though it's been a hell of a lot longer than that, and I just think this supposed dream job has definitely turned into a nightmare."

Floyd nodded as he smiled. "It's not the easiest job in the world, Todd, that's definitely true. It may pay a lot—much more than it should, I think—but there's a lot of shit you need to put up with. I put up with all of that crap for 35 years. Looking back, I honestly don't know how I did it."

"And just succeeding you in such a short period of time, I honestly don't know how I'm still hanging on. It's like I dreamed of getting this job, and I only know I got it because I was the creator of the Royce Voice, which you know is now defunct."

"I know," he replied, and took a sip of his tea.

"But I'm seeing firsthand the reality of actually working for the Royce family. It's not all what people think it is. I thought I was on top of the world at that press conference when I was announced as the new spokesman and when they threw that party for me later on that night. But my wife has always thought from the beginning that something was never right."

"Well, I can't blame Kasi. I wish I had a wife like her. Due to my job, I never married. It's just been me and my mom. Sure, I had a lot of girlfriends, and I was even engaged once, but nothing came out of it. I told them that my life was devoted to my job. Now I wish I would've gotten someone back then. Now I'm sitting here with no one but my mom, which is fine with her."

Todd laughed as he took a sip of his water. "I just don't know what to do, man."

Floyd's eyes lit up in curiosity. "You're thinking about resigning?"

"It crossed my mind because Kasi is worried about my well-being, but I'm being paid millions a year to give press conferences about the Royce family as well as other things. We're living in a house similar to this one all because of my job. I knew that talking about them was one thing, but working for them was going to be a whole different thing, but I didn't know it was gonna be this much stress this soon."

"Well, you saw in the last years how it was when I worked for them. They were by far the worse, especially after Dray met Eve and they got married. I'm not saying it's Eve's fault since she married into the family, but it's been one fucked-up thing after another. I hated to say it, but when it was confirmed that Clayton fired me, and Mayson approved of it, I felt some relief. But I also was very distraught because I knew I no longer had a job and had to completely disassociate myself from the Royce family. I haven't had a job since, and luckily that due to investments I made with their company that I am financially wealthy that I don't have to work and can pay for the care of my mom."

"That's good, Floyd. So, I hate to put you on the spot, but how do you think I've done with giving press conferences? Is it similar in style to the way you gave them?"

"You mean you've never seen me give one?"

"Yes, I've seen you give a lot of them. I just wanted to know am I as good?"

"You're just fine, Todd. I don't think the Royces would've hired you if they didn't think you could do the job like the way I did. We both have different delivery techniques unique to us, and what works for you works well like what worked for me worked well. I'm just gonna say that I don't think you should quit working for them. It might be the best job you ever get. You have stock options with them as well like what I had, and you're making a hell of a lot more money than I made when I first started there. It was a massive step up from being a fast-food manager."

"Wow, I didn't know that's what you did before you became the Royce spokesman. That was definitely a big step up, man," Todd said, as he took a sip of his drink as he stared at him in curiosity.

"Sometimes we can get very lucky in life," Floyd said, as he stared back at him while taking another sip of his tea.

"Yeah, and in a lot of ways I felt I did because they told me that they had thousands of applicants who applied for your job, but they gave the job to me. I felt there were a lot of others who were definitely more qualified than me."

"There definitely were," Floyd replied, and took another sip of his tea. "But even more were definitely more qualified than me."

Todd tried to suppress an offended look. "Why did Prentiss Willoughby resign? Do you know?"

Floyd took another sip of his tea. "Yes."

Todd's interest was piqued. "I'm listening, man."

"Look, man, you have to promise me that you won't say anything, okay? I'm really not supposed to be talking about the Royces to you since I'm a fired employee and you're a current one, and especially since you have the job now that I should still have."

"I'm listening, man," Todd said again, and took another quick sip of his drink.

"Prentiss quit because he couldn't take any more of the secrets, lies, and bullshit."

"For real?" Todd asked. "I know this was decades ago, but what happened?"

"He feels that Mayson definitely knew that it was Lulu who poisoned one of his mistresses to death back in the 1950s, and he was going to go to the cops about it but decided against it because after all, he had absolutely no proof of it. He needed his job and told me it was the best job he'd ever had; same thing you and I have said. But I think it was just everything that'd happened during his time there and he'd seen enough. The Royce men are bullies, Todd. They think they can get away with anything, and I mean anything, and this started with the late Grayson Royce. They're the cause of so much shit, I can't even begin to get started on it. It actually amazes me that they have gotten as far and as wealthy in their lives because of it. But Prentiss told me before he left that I inherited a mess, but he wouldn't tell me what the mess was, until I did what you're doing right now—I asked could I talk to him alone about his job and why he resigned, when like me—and like you—he had full and total tenure. Being a Royce spokesman is no joke, and I know you know that by now, Todd."

"I most definitely do, Floyd. It sounds like a lot of shit has been going on since the Royce family has been in existence. They seem to have gotten away with a lot of shit as well because of their wealthy status. But who can prove they have been the cause of these things that have happened? I would like to think that they're not."

"Me too, Todd. But that's a lot of wishful thinking on our parts. A lot of shit goes on in every family, but the Royces are on a whole other level, as you know. They made you sign a book of contracts like I know they made me sign when I accepted the job from them, but little did we all know is that they had a book just as big of the shit they've caused with all of their secrets and lies inside of them."

"Damn, that's deep, Floyd. Now I'm really starting to see what I signed up for, and it's not good."

"It's been never good, Todd. But in my case, it was better than being a manager at a fast-food restaurant. I was working for one of the richest Black families in the world, now confirmed to be the richest in the world and have been for years and years. I was living a dream life beyond my dreams, but the job was a nightmare."

"And you're not lying there. I guess when you're on the outside of something you desire to be like, it's like you'll do anything to be on the inside. And I admit that's how I was. My wife has actually been against me taking this job from the start. She said she's never liked the Royces because of all of the shit they've caused, and they always seem to go unpunished and unscathed because of it. I mean, Leon was almost killed at Dray and Eve's wedding protecting her, but when they were shot at constantly, they never got hit."

"Yeah, funny how that works out, huh? But Leon was a fool to go back working for them. He must really be in love with Eve even though he's now officially married."

"And I admit that I have seen their intimacy in person."

Floyd's eyes got big. "You did?"

"Yeah, I accidentally walked in on them at that Sexy Six party. He pulled a fuckin' gun out on me and told me to get the fuck out of there. All I was doing was my job of checking the Royces' private rooms to make sure no one was in them, but Eve was in hers getting hammered by Leon. Right then and there, I knew that not everything was perfect in their family, and they were always hiding a lot of shit. I felt I was meant to see what I saw. And would you believe that Dray made Eve say she was sorry to me for what I'd seen?"

"Really?"

"At that moment, I really felt sorry for her because I felt he embarrassed and humiliated her by making her apologize to me, but he didn't make Leon apologize to me."

"Yeah, that's interesting. I never caught Miriam doing anything with anyone, and neither did I catch Clayton, even though I know he's cheated on her a million times with a million different women. Boy, I always dreamed of having a wife as beautiful as her, and thought all the time that Clayton took her for granted—and I still do. But I feel it's just gonna get worse with the Royces and them being the cause of shit, so you need to prepare yourself for it."

"That's if I'm still employed by them."

"So you're really thinking about quitting this fast, huh?" Floyd said, and took another sip of his tea.

"Kasi really wants me to, but if I do, I just don't know what I'm gonna do. I've been there for just a very tiny fraction of the time you were there, and I've seen enough already to last me a lifetime, and now I think about how long you were there and what you saw during your time on the job, and now you tell me that the worst is yet to come?"

"Well, I shouldn't say that, Todd. I guess I am still a little enviable that I no longer work for them because it was an unexpected firing and in a lot of ways I thought I would be forgiven by them by now and would've been offered a demoted job or something—but they were serious as I knew that they were. I committed a very serious infraction that was a firing offense. I have no one to blame but myself. I just have to take my early retirement like a man which is what I've been doing and watch from afar all of the things that the Royce family have done and know that I no longer have anything to do with any of it. My time with them is done, and I'm the cause of it."

Todd looked at his watch. "Well, I hate to cut this short because this is the most interesting and informative conversation I've ever had, and I didn't think you were gonna accept my wanting to talk to you about my current job and your former job. It's been very eye-opening, and I would like to find out a lot more and a lot more about Prentiss and his time doing this job as well."

"I'll tell you anything you wanna know. All of this just has to stay between us because I know the Royces would not like it at all if they knew you were talking to me."

"I know they wouldn't."

They walked to the front door.

The doorbell rang.

They looked at each other.

"Are you expecting anyone?" Todd asked as he gave a guarded look.

"No, I'm not. I was only expecting you," he replied, as he slowly walked towards his front door with Todd by his side. He opened it.

"Hello, Floyd Ferguson."

"Hello," Floyd replied.

"In case you forget who I am, I'm Detective Bruce Cook, this is my partner Detective Armond Howell. We're here because we would like to ask you questions about the 40-year-old cold case murder of Jolene Woodburn."

CHAPTER 30

THE STORM

"So, Auer, how do you feel about Leon being back?" Dray asked, as he drove him home from a business meeting while a light rain came falling from the night sky while flashes of lightning put on a show.

"I'm glad he's back. I think he's a great bodyguard for your wife and son. He told me he never even thought about leaving, he just needed that self-care, that's all."

"Yeah, that female shit," Dray said with a grin, as he leaned his head back on the headrest. "You still fucking Carmella, man?"

"Yeah, we're still doing it. Is that okay?"

"Anything to get your rocks off, man. Y'all ain't serious about each other, are you?"

"I'm not serious about her, hell naw. She's nasty as fuck."

"But she better not be doing any of that nasty-as-fuck shit in the presence of my daughter."

"We don't, man. Stormy is in another room all of the time, and I always make sure of it."

"Good looking out, man, because sometimes I just don't know about that chick."

"She's all right, man. She really loves Stormy and takes great care of her."

"She knows she better or else I would've found someone else by now." He laid his head back even more. "Damn!" He wildly shifted in all directions in his seat and let out a load moan that shook the car.

"How was that?" Sia said!

"You did that shit better than my wife, baby," he said.

Auer looked in the rearview mirror; he shook his head.

"Wow, what a compliment. Thanks," she said with a big smile. She wiped her mouth with a towel. "Can I get that big, beautiful dick inside me now?"

"Not now, Sia. I have to get home. Eve is waiting for me," Dray said, as he stared out the window. He looked at his phone. "Stop the car, Auer! Stop the car!"

"What? What is it?" Sia asked.

Auer immediately pulled over to the side.

"Get the fuck out," he said to Sia!

"What? What do you mean get the fuck out, Dray! It's raining! We're out in the middle of nowhere!"

"You got your phone, get the fuck out right now or I'm gonna have Auer throw you out!" Dray said.

"What the fuck is wrong with you all of the sudden?!" she asked in a whiny voice.

"I SAID GET THE FUCK OUT! AUER!"

Auer was ready to open his door.

"Okay! I'll get out! What the fuck is wrong with you, Dray! I don't know where the fuck I am!" She got her purse and opened the door and got out.

Auer immediately sped off after she shut the door. She looked at the black Rolls-Royce Phantom until it disappeared out of sight. She sighed as she began walking up the road as she got on her phone to call a friend.

No answer.

She tried numerous people, but didn't want to try the most obvious person because she didn't want to have to answer any questions about how she got out on the middle of a deserted road and she wasn't driving her car. "Leon is gonna fuckin' kill me if he finds out I'm out here."

The rain started to come down at an even heavier pace as lightning danced in the night sky and loud claps of thunder shook the ground. It was completely dark out on this narrow road, and there was no light of a nearest intersection in sight.

Sia walked up the street as her phone was glued to her ear as she tried desperately to get in touch with any of her friends or relatives, and still no answer from any of them. A pair of bright headlights appeared behind her. She turned around as the rain continued to come down as hard as the sky was still putting on a show of lightning with earsplitting sounds of thunder throughout it.

The window rolled down on the passenger's side. "Want a ride?"

She wasn't sure.

"Come on. Get in. I'll take you wherever you need to go. It's storming bad out here and it's way too dark and dangerous regardless."

Everything she was taught about never getting in the car with a stranger was an afterthought at this very moment. She got in and closed the door. "Thank you."

"You're welcome. There's a towel in the back seat if you wanna dry yourself off."

She reached back and got the towel. "Thanks."

"What were you doing out here all by yourself?"

She sighed. "I wasn't out here by myself at first. I got kicked out of someone's car."

"In this weather? Wow, it must've been serious."

"For him it was; at least that's what he told me. He told me it was so serious that I had to get out and find another way home because he had to immediately get somewhere."

"Who? May I ask?"

She sighed once again. "Dray. Dray Royce. Do you know him?"

"Everyone knows the Royces."

Auer drove up to Clayton and Miriam's home . . . and to a plethora amount of cop cars as well as ambulances. Dray jumped out of the car before Auer came to a complete stop as I came running towards him.

"DRAY!!!! OH MY GOD! OH MY GOD!" I said as I cried as hard as the rain coming down.

"EVE! What's wrong, baby? What is it?! WHAT?!" he yelled as he held on to my shoulders as he was trying to shake it out of me.

Leon went over to Auer to tell him what was going on.

"My dad, Dray! My dad!" I cried.

"Your dad? Eve, what's wrong with your dad, baby? What's going on?"

"My dad!" I said as I cried even harder.

"Eve! WHAT?! Talk to me, baby! What about your dad?!"

I started to hyperventilate as I leaned over. He held on to me as he straightened me up enough to look at him.

"What about your dad, Eve?"

"My dad . . . MY DAD *SHOT YOUR DAD!*"

BILLIONAIRE
Dray Royce
SERIES
WHEN THE
PAST BECOMES
UNCOVERED ...
TENTH IN THE
SERIES
COVERING
FROM
Dray
SHEILA
MURDOCK

ABOUT THE AUTHOR

Sheila Murdock is a combination of her birth name and her late grandmother's maiden name on her mother's side.

When she's not writing, she enjoys watching movies and TV shows—old and new—on YouTube, Netflix, and Amazon Prime Video, but always loves a surprising show she can find on cable TV. She also enjoys reading all kinds of non-fiction, but has a particular interest in African-American historical and contemporary non-fiction, but will read an occasional fiction book. She enjoys listening to old-school/throwback rap, hip-hop, and R&B, and jazz music from any era.